OUT OF ORDER

OUT OF ORDER

A. M. JENKINS

HARPERCOLLINS*PUBLISHERS*

Thanks to the members of the Four Star Coffee Bar Critique Group and the YAWRITER listserve, for writerly opinions and moral support; especially Catherine Atkins, David Davis, Debra Deur, Janet Fick, Lisa Firke, Chris Ford, Judy Gregerson, Shirley Harazin, Lisa Harkrader, Jim Janik, Kathy Lay, Martha Moore, Jennifer Page, Jan Peck, Diane Roberts, Melissa Russell, Andrea Schulz, B. J. Stone, Shelley Sykes, Sue Ward, Laura Wiess, Nancy Werlin, Cerelle Woods, and Melissa Wyatt.

Library of Congress Cataloging-in-Publication Data
Jenkins, A. M. (Amanda McRaney)
  Out of order / by A. M. Jenkins.— 1st ed.
    p.   cm.
  Summary: Sophomore Colt Trammel loves baseball and his girlfriend Grace, but he hates the rest of high school and maintains a tough facade to hide his feelings of inferiority.
  ISBN 0-06-623968-0 — ISBN 0-06-623969-9 (lib. bdg.)
  [1. High school—Fiction. 2. Schools—Fiction. 3. Interpersonal relations—Fiction. 4. Self-perception—Fiction.] I. Title.
PZ7.J41315 Ou 2003   2002015621
[Fic]—dc21
CIP
AC

Typography by Hilary Zarycky
3 4 5 6 7 8 9 10
❖
First Edition

To Alix and Steve,
for putting my future back into my hands

WEEK ONE

CHAPTER ONE

A Graceless Day

I'm in a bad mood, walking into first-period biology. If I had my books, I'd slam them on the lab table.

But I don't have them. They're in the bottom of my locker where I left them. I don't feel like doing any work today.

I slump down in my seat. I fold my arms over my chest. I don't laugh or talk to anybody, and everybody who has eyes can see not to mess with me.

I don't have a lab partner. Eddie DiCicco used to be it, but after I got caught copying off one of his labs, Ms. Keller moved him. Now I sit alone, which means every time we have a test, I've got to write all the answers down myself, on a cheat sheet.

I hate Ms. Keller.

The bell rings. Everybody's already in place, because Ms. Keller counts you tardy if you're not in your seat when the bell rings. Everybody's getting their books out, because Ms. Keller makes you read a couple pages while she's checking the roll.

It takes her about two seconds to see that I'm not reading. "Colt. Where's your book?"

"I don't have it." If she'll give me a pass to my locker, I might just take a detour and not come back for a while. I'm not in the mood for looking at plant cells today.

Ms. Keller doesn't say anything about a pass. Instead she makes a mark in her grade book. It's a zero, for not coming to class prepared.

She doesn't offer to let me use one of the extras in her desk. I guess I get to read the assignment for homework.

Fuck her, anyway.

She starts writing the day's assignment on the overhead. I've got nothing to read, so I have to just sit and wait. That's supposed to be more punishment. It could be punishment, if I start thinking about how I blew it with Grace last night.

Better get my mind on something else. I lean back to balance my chair on two legs, almost to the point of falling. I try to think about anything besides you-know-who.

Baseball. I'm very good at baseball. Baseball is the only part of my life I have any control over. Baseball is the only reason I'm still in school.

4

Problem: I'm not out on the field. I'm in here. There's no way you can think about baseball when your body's trapped on a hard chair in a quiet room, and you can't move at all. When you can't feel the shock of the bat running up your arm into your shoulder. When you can't feel the *whump!* of the ball in your glove.

When the girl you've been in love with since seventh grade walked off mad, and as usual she's going to stay that way till you crawl like a dog.

But God, I'm so crazy about her. I want everybody to say "ColtandGrace" the way they say "RomeoandJuliet" or "RickyandLucy."

I remember middle school, when Grace and I had seventh-grade social studies together, and I'd be sitting two desks back and one desk over. And I remember whenever we had to write an essay, instead of working on my essay, I'd sit and watch Grace write. She always wore this tiny little bracelet, so thin and gold I could have snapped it with my breath. And her arm would be moving back and forth, back and forth, back and forth over the paper, and all these ideas would be flowing down through her hand and pouring out the pen, so smooth, with no effort, and it made me not ever want to pick up *my* goddamn pen again.

And if the sun was just right, coming in the windows, I could see tiny golden soft hairs on her forearm. And sometimes she'd turn her head and stare off to the side, out the window, and I could almost see all those ideas rolling around in there, inside that head.

I'm thinking about this, and I'm even almost forgetting I'm in biology, when the classroom door opens. A person—a girl, probably, though it's not easy to tell—comes in. She's got green hair. Or partly; about three or four inches of roots are regular hair color. But the rest is definitely green. It's parted in the middle, and cut straight on the bottom, just below her chin. If it wasn't for those unmistakable boobs under the sweat jacket, she could be a skinny, underdeveloped guy.

Everybody's reading silently. Ms. Keller sits at her desk, checking off the roll. Her eyes flick over me, tilted back in my chair. She's given up trying to get me to stop doing that—now she's just hoping I'll fall so she can say I told you so.

Sorry, not gonna happen.

The girl gives Ms. Keller a white slip. Ms. Keller reaches into the big bottom drawer of her desk and hands the girl a textbook.

Oh, sure. *I* get a zero, but this chick gets a book.

"Take that seat right there," Ms. Keller says.

She's pointing at the seat next to me.

"You can share your book with Colt. He seems to have forgotten his this morning."

The girl tucks the book under her arm—just like a guy—and heads my way. She's wearing running shoes and boys' jeans, and when she unzips her sweat jacket, I see she's got on a Hawaiian shirt, only instead of flowers it's got cats doing the hula all over it.

I hate weird people. And poor people and sick people, for that matter. They all give me a bad feeling, like This Could Be You Instead of Me.

The girl ties her sweat jacket around her waist and sits beside me. She glances at the page numbers on the board and opens her book. She slides the book halfway between us without bothering to look up.

I don't even pretend to lean over and read.

Why do people think they can dress any way they want? Don't they see that they're outsiders for a reason? That they bring it on themselves by not being and dressing and acting within the rules? Don't they know there's an order to things, and once you step out of the order, you're fair game? Instead all you get is whining about how they're picked on. Shit, if they're that stupid, they deserve to get picked on, is all I've got to say.

Like Alicia Doggett, who sits across the room. One thing you can say about Alicia is that she knows where she stands. She's like a chihuahua cringing and blinking its way around the school, so you don't notice her unless you're really, really bored. She'd drop dead from fear or joy if she had to share a book with Colt Trammel.

But this new girl doesn't know who I am, and she's dressed like the roofers that reshingled our house after the last hailstorm. And she strolled down the aisle like it doesn't even matter.

I've got to tell you, that whole attitude sends smart-ass remarks boiling up my throat.

The girl turns a page without even checking to see if I'm done reading it.

The door opens a crack, and Ms. Keller gets called to the door by some unknown loser. So when she's standing in the doorway talking, I ask the girl next to me, "What happened to your hair?" And I stare at it, like something alive just crawled out.

She just gives me this look, like I'm an idiot.

"So," I say, conversational. "You must be from Greenland."

"And you must be from Uranus," she says, in a you're-an-idiot voice. She doesn't know who I am—she's new and she doesn't know girls with bad dye jobs and stupid clothes can't talk back to people like me.

I'll teach her. "I gotta ask you something," I add. "Be honest, now. You *are* a girl, aren't you?"

"Screw you," Greenland says, under her breath.

"You wish," I tell her.

"No way," she shoots back. "I prefer men, not dickless little boys."

"Honey, I'll show you a dick," I say. "I'll show you a dick times *ten*." I reach for my belt, like I'm really going to whip it out right in biology.

She makes a big show of propping her elbow on the lab table and staring at my fly, like she can't wait for me to exhibit my one-eyed general.

I'm kind of stuck. I've gone too far again. I don't want to back down, but I can't really pull it out in the middle of class, either.

I don't look around. That would be uncool. I keep my eyes on her face, and I reach for my belt. She's really zeroed in on my crotch. I feel a little uncomfortable, having a girl stare at it like she's expecting some kind of performing poodle.

Nice and easy, I slide the end of my belt through the leather loop. Then—snap! I pop it open, so the metal prong is pointing right at her.

She just smirks. Like, go ahead—I dare you.

I dart a glance around. Behind us Haley Turner is looking on the way my sister watches surgeons cut people's heads open on PBS. Her lab partner, Michael McMillan, is grinning. He really thinks I'm going to do it.

Am I? I don't know. It'd go down in history. It'd be

remembered years from now, when the proms and football games are nothing but pictures in the yearbook. The year Colt Trammel paraded his prick in sophomore biology.

Greenland is still waiting, watching. Yeah, she's smirking now, but what's she going to do if I really go through with it? Scream? Call Ms. Keller? Sue the school district? Have me arrested?

Better yet, maybe she'll ask to be moved to a different seat.

I slip the leather end completely out of the buckle. I pull it wide open. I can feel myself smirking back at her.

I think I'm going to do it.

"Colton Trammel," calls Ms. Keller. "We're on page thirty-seven. You want to join us?"

Greenland and I both look up.

My chance for glory is gone. I scoot my chair up and try to figure out where we are on the page.

"Read the boxed comments out loud for us please, Colt," Ms. Keller says. "Corinne, help him find the place."

Greenland/Corinne points to a bunch of words boxed in by a black line.

"Chulrofile," I begin.

"Chlorophyll," corrects Ms. Keller.

"Chlorophyll is the green pig-ment found in the . . ."

"Chloroplasts," says Ms. Keller.

". . . of plant cells," I finish. Deep breath. Next sentence.

Greenland is leaning to read over my arm, chin on her hand, her green hair curling slightly against her fingers. I can feel my open belt, under the table. I can't take the time now to fasten it up. When I'm reading, it always takes all my concentration not to stumble over the words. Even more so today, what with the near flashing and all. Plus, I didn't sleep so good last night.

Not after what happened with Grace.

"I love you," I whispered against her neck.

We were in my car, in a parking lot, and things were getting pretty heavy, so heavy that I swear I was about to pass out from breathing too fast, because my face was buried in her hair, and I could smell her, just Grace, her shampoo, lotion, whatever it is, a smell no one would ever know unless he had his face against her like I did, and for the first time one of my hands was actually working its way under her skirt without any interference. Grace was allowing it. And that's why I couldn't stand it anymore and said, "I love you."

And that's when her hands stopped moving in my hair. "You *what*?"

I knew I'd done something wrong.

But how could "I love you" be wrong?

I tried again. I held perfectly still and said it again. Only it came out as a question. "I love you?"

She didn't move either. But when she spoke, her voice was like an icy street, where you'd better drive slow if you don't want to end up in a ditch. "You've never said that before."

"So?" I asked.

As soon as it came out, I knew it was wrong. *So?* Definitely not in the spirit of the moment.

"So *now* you love me. Not when we're sitting and talking. Just when you think you're going to *get* something out of it."

Now I understood. We were in the front seat of my car, and after months—months!—I was about to get somewhere. *Anything* would have been the wrong thing to say. Even "I love you."

I tried again, anyway. "But I *do* love you."

Bzzzzzzt. Wrong answer.

Grace pushed me away and scrambled to sit up. "You don't love me. You don't even understand me." She pulled her skirt down. "If you did, you wouldn't have lied the other day about how much you liked my poem."

"Oh, *God*," I said, and fell back to my side of the car. "Not again! Not *now!*"

"You love me—right! If you loved me, you'd know how important my writing is to me, and you wouldn't have lied about it." She tugged the front of her blouse back into place. "All that bull about how you treasured my poem. I saw how much you treasured it! *You used it for a coaster!*"

I banged my forehead on the steering wheel a couple of times. No point in answering.

She slid her hands up underneath her shirt, and I knew she was putting her bra back where it belonged, doing it all out of sight, so I couldn't see.

"You just want me to put out," she muttered.

"No." I said it out loud. I was going to make this work. "I mean it," I told her. "I *do* want you to put out, but I also love you." The whole truth, and nothing but the truth, for Grace. "I've always loved you. I love you more than I've ever loved anybody." I spilled it all, for the first time ever. Which left me feeling barefoot surrounded by broken glass.

"Stop saying that." Grace reached inside her neckline to adjust something. Then she sat back. Grace always has a lot of words, the right words, there at her fingertips. "Take me home," she ordered.

Go figure, a girl getting mad because you say you love her.

But she didn't say that she didn't want to see me anymore.

Not yet.

And we'd been down this road before. I always manage to tiptoe back. I'm a bad habit that Grace can't quite kick. Always trying to make myself into a good habit, so she won't *want* to kick me.

"Okay," I whispered—funny how your voice shakes when you know one more single wrong word could blow your whole world away.

I'd never driven so carefully in my life. I'd just laid myself out at her feet. She knew everything. Almost.

And all the way to her house I was thinking, maybe if I tell her *that*, too, she'll understand that I really do love her.

Or maybe she wouldn't believe *that*, either.

When I got to her house, I stopped the engine. Before I could even move, she was out the door and heading up the sidewalk.

I got out anyway. I didn't follow her, I just stood looking over the car, resting my elbows on the roof, watching to see that she made it to the door.

Her strappy little sandals made angry slaps on the concrete. I was probably the only person in the world who noticed she had her toenails painted pink. Her calves were bare—I knew her legs were bare, though they were only a blurry dark movement under the gauze of her skirt, against the porch light.

"Hey," I tried, calling out so suddenly that it surprised

my vocal cords and came out as a croak. "You're right. I'm a liar. I don't love you. Okay?"

It didn't fix anything. She didn't look around. Didn't say anything, either. The front door wasn't locked—she just opened it and walked in. She didn't slam it but shut it firmly.

"See you tomorrow," I whispered, even though I knew that nobody could hear me. Because tomorrow I'd work hard and get her to soften up and give me one of those smiles that flashed the message for the whole world to see:

Colton Trammel is somebody special.

I waited, elbows resting on the car roof, until I made sure she got in okay. And when the door shut behind her, I pounded the roof with my fist: one, two, three. Just to get under control enough to crawl back in the car and drive off, so I didn't go up and knock on her front door and say something stupid like the rest of the truth. That I, Colt Trammel, Studly Hombre, have never gone all the way. Right up to the edge, but I've never tasted the whole tuna taco.

Because I've always wanted Grace to be my first.

When you're in love with somebody and they're mad at you, two things happen. One is that every second hurts. If you weren't in love, you never would have noticed these seconds passing, but now you can feel every single miserable one of them, like you ate some bad chicken enchiladas at a Tex-Mex buffet.

The second thing is that you are being pulled against your will toward the person you love, like a moth to a bug zapper. For example, even though I haven't seen her all day, I know exactly where Grace is, and I can feel every inch of space between us trying to get smaller.

As I'm walking to fourth-period English, I know that she's just on the other side of the school—down the hall, turn left, cross the breezeway, left again, through the double doors on the right—that's the cafeteria where *she's* sitting down with her little brown lunch sack. I know she's there, eating and talking and breathing.

Of course, I can't even think about going to see her, because if I think about it, I'll end up doing it. And deep down, I know exactly what I really need to do about Grace. I know—I'm just not sure I can manage.

Because what I've got to do is . . . nothing. Stay away from her; let her be the one to crawl first, for a change. That's the smart thing. After all, most people would say that *she's* the one who's not good enough for *me*. I mean, Grace is good-looking—but I am too. It's a simple fact: I'm a stud. I've been out with plenty of other girls, while I'm the only guy Grace's ever dated. So I know a lot of stuff, while she's lived a pretty protected life, guywise. Her dad's real strict, so she couldn't even go on a real date till she turned fifteen. Her first date was me, her second date was me, all the dates she's ever had have been me. I'm all she knows.

There's no need to break down and call her like I always do. No point in humiliating myself by hunting her down at school. She'll come around, if I can just lay off.

I go on to fourth period alone, walk in the classroom, sit down. My desk is by the window because I do better in wide-open spaces. Or at least next to them.

The bell rings. Mr. Hammond walks in a moment later. Damn. If there was any mercy in the universe, we'd have a substitute today.

Mr. Hammond's okay, as far as teachers go. His only bad point is that he hasn't cut me any slack yet. My mom about had a stroke when she saw that 68 he gave me for the first six weeks.

Grades aside, Mr. Hammond's got some good points. He doesn't call my mom and complain about me. He lets me run errands for him, which most teachers don't once they get to know me. He doesn't say stuff like "This is *easy*, Colt, it's *simple*," so that I feel like an asshole when I don't get it.

So I like Hammond okay, and though I'm not doing

too good in here at the moment, I have hopes that he won't play hardball when the next progress reports come out.

"Open your books to page ninety-seven—'The Chimney Sweeper,' by William Blake," Mr. Hammond says. "I think you all are going to like this one."

He starts reading it out loud, with lots of pauses and expression. Grace would love it, all that expression in his voice. Me, I think it's pitiful. A grown man devoting his whole life to trying to get teenagers to care about literature.

It's hard to watch sometimes, how bad Mr. Hammond wants everybody to love this stuff, this English stuff. Sometimes I think how happy he'd be if he could have a bunch of students like Grace in here, who'd appreciate all his hard work.

Because to a guy like me "The Chimney Sweeper" is some piece of shit. It doesn't make a bit of sense. Of course, it would to those High Academic Program types. They'd take one look at it and see the secret meaning that Mr. Hammond has to explain to the rest of us, that it's about boys who clean chimneys for a living.

He says how the boys are like lambs. As in baby sheep. That's right . . . baby sheep. It doesn't *say* that, of course; you're just supposed to *know*.

"What are some words in the poem that could be associated with lambs?" Hammond is asking.

"His hair curls like a lamb's back," some girl says.

"Yes!" Mr. Hammond's fist pounds the desk. He's like one of those motivational speakers. "Any others?"

He looks around the room. Everybody else is like me; nobody raises a hand, nobody makes a sound.

Still, Hammond waits, like if he gives us a little thinking time, we'll all suddenly turn into geniuses.

"Look at the verbs," he hints after a moment.

Still nothing. It's so quiet, I can actually hear a cricket chirping outside.

"If you saw a group of lambs out in a field, what kinds of things would they be doing?"

The girl next to me yawns so wide, her jaw creaks.

Hammond's in a tailspin, poor guy. I feel sorry for him—I'm having a bad day too; I know how it feels.

So now I take a look for some lamb words in case it might cheer him up to see me looking. And God, can you imagine if I was actually the one who found a lamb word? He'd retire on the spot. He'd have reached the peak of teacherhood.

I'm looking for something like "Baaa," I guess, but there's nothing there. Just regular words.

"What about 'down a green plain leaping, laughing, they run'?" Mr. Hammond presses. "'And wash in a river, and shine in the sun'—they used to wash sheep by taking them to the river. Once the sheep were clean, they'd take them in for shearing. Look at the fifth stanza; 'Then naked and white—'"

I perk up a little at the word *naked*, and find it on the page.

"'—all their bags left behind, / They rise upon clouds and sport in the wind.' How do you think a sheep would feel, to be rid of all that heavy fleece? What do you think it would do, once the shearers released it?"

Silence in the classroom. It's like the man is speaking a different language. Nobody has any idea what he just said.

"To 'sport'—what does that mean?" Hammond asks, but this time he gives up and answers himself. "To frolic, or play. Can't you see the lambs frolicking, playing once they're relieved of their burdens? 'Sport in the wind'?"

He quits with the questions and starts talking again. About child labor laws or something. I like him okay, but I hate this class. English has always been a nightmare to me. It's a battle for me to stay in regular and not get stuck in remedial. I've always kept ahead of the game, but I still hate English, I hate books, I hate school in general. Always have. Any minute somebody could be expecting you to read out loud, or to explain something.

"Mr. Trammel," Mr. Hammond says. "How do you think you'd feel, spending all your days inside dark, cramped chimneys, breathing soot and coal dust?"

"Like Santa Claus."

A couple of giggles behind me. Mr. Hammond just looks at me and waits. Unlike all the other English teachers I've ever had, he only asks me stuff I can answer.

So I give in. "Bad," I tell him. "I'd feel bad."

"That's right," agrees Mr. Hammond, nodding. Then he moves on, going off on another subject, *blah blah blah, blah blah blah*. And after a while I forget to try to listen, and look outside. I'd rather be someplace that doesn't have a ceiling or floor, where the air is fresh and not canned. I'd rather be anywhere, walking around or running or hitting balls, than be in here having to sit in the same place and keep my comments to myself and my hands and feet still.

Hammond's on the other side of the room, still talking. I pick up my pencil, hunch over my folder so my body looks like I'm taking notes.

The grass outside is the same color as honey. The sky's got no clouds, it's blue like the soft little sweater Grace wore last night, the one with no sleeves.

I wish I could not care about her at all. Just until she gets over being mad.

Anybody besides me, he'd have already moved on— or he'd be able to at least act like he had.

It ought to be easy to move on. Grace wouldn't know how to flirt if you handed her written instructions. Her number-one handicap is that she's very intellectual and serious-minded.

Me, I *do* know how to flirt, and I'm about as unserious and unintellectual as you can get. I can hardly keep up with all her bullshit talk about writing and books and movies, excuse me, *films*.

Maybe that's why I've got to prove to myself and everybody else that I can have her.

A hand gently comes down on my pencil—and I realize I've been tapping it on the desk. *Ratta-tat, ratta-tat, ratta-tat.* Like a very small machine gun.

"'He was energy itself,'" Mr. Hammond's voice booms, because he's the one looming above me—Pay attention, Colt!

I put my pencil down and Mr. Hammond's hand leaves, but he stays there, inches from my desk, reading from the piece of paper in his hand. "'. . . and shed around him a kindling influence, an atmosphere of life.'"

He always does this—somehow he knows when I'm not really paying attention, so he brings his lecture over right in front of my desk.

"'He was a man,'" Mr. Hammond reads off the printout, "'without a mask.'"

I do what I always do—I stare right at him, so nobody

knows I have no clue what he's talking about, and nobody can complain how I'm not paying attention. It's an old trick—just look the teacher right between the eyes, just keep your own eyes glued to that one spot on the bridge of their nose, and then your mind can wander wherever it wants.

Where my mind wants to wander is Grace.

That's the story of my life. The same thing's always going to happen. No matter what I do or don't do, I'm always going to end up right back where I started, with Grace stuck inside me like an arrowhead broken off the whatdyacallit. The stick part with the feathers.

Fifth period, I'm an assistant. That means instead of taking a regular class, you sign up to help some teacher; grading papers, running errands, whatever. Usually you have to be an honor-roll student before you get to be somebody's assistant, but Coach Kline talked Miss A., who teaches English, into taking me on. Coach knows I don't do too good in some of my classes, and his thinking was that I could use this time as a study hall, plus get help from Miss A. if I need it.

At first I thought it was cool. Not only would I have a free hall pass, but Miss A. also teaches journalism, so I get to be all by myself in this little room that joins Miss A.'s classroom. It's the one where the newspaper staff has their meetings. There's a door that opens out into the hall, and there's also a phone in here.

It's not so cool now. There's usually nothing to do because Miss A. doesn't let me run errands anymore. Not since the time she sent me to the attendance office and I forgot to come back. And it turns out the hall door's always locked to keep people from coming in and messing with the newspaper stuff, so I can't sneak out. And I'm not supposed to use the phone; Miss A. caught me the only time I tried, and she told Coach and he made me run laps during sixth.

After that, Coach said he'd bench me if Miss A. complained one more time, and maybe even get me moved to a real class instead of assistant.

My guess is Coach Kline and Miss A. have a thing going, but I haven't gotten up the nerve to ask.

Now I mostly just put my head down and sleep in here. Nobody bothers me, except every once in a while Miss A. has some homework she wants me to grade. She won't let me grade tests, although I'm good at that—I like checking off other people's mistakes.

Today, as usual, nothing to do. I put my head down on my arms. I like this room, even if those High Academic Program types do work and write in it. It's in the old part of the building, the part that was built back before sheetrock and particle board, so it has a little personality. There's wooden cabinets all around the walls, ceiling to floor, and the floors are wood, too, and the air smells like musty shellac. It's cozy, too—the sun comes straight in the windows and the only thing moving is the dust in the sunbeams.

It's a great place to sleep. Usually.

Today I've just shut my eyes when I hear the door to Miss A.'s classroom open.

"Colt, you have a helper," she says.

No sleeping today. I raise my head and take a good look at my "helper."

It's Greenland. "Oh, great," I say, and drop my head back down on my arms.

"This is Corinne," I hear Miss A. say. I don't look up. There's a pause, where Miss A.'s deciding whether it's worth the time involved to make me sit up and be polite.

She decides it's not worth it. "Corinne, the gentleman with the fine manners is Colt Trammel."

"We've met," I hear Greenland say, in this voice that makes it clear we didn't exactly hit it off.

"Good," says Miss A., grimly. "Then you know what to expect. Just have a seat anywhere."

There's the slow squeak of footsteps coming over to the table, and a chair screeching back on the wood floor.

"I don't really have anything for you two to work on

today," Miss A. adds. "Can you wisely handle some free time?"

I don't have to see her to know she's aiming that at me.

"I've got some homework I can do," Greenland tells her.

"Good. Colt," Miss A. presses, because I haven't answered, "you doing all right?"

What she means is, you do anything bad and I'll tell my boyfriend and he'll bench your butt.

"Yeah, I'm all right." I mumble it at the tabletop.

Miss A.'s little heels *click click click* out of the room. The door shuts.

I hear the *thunk!* of a backpack hitting the tabletop. A zipping sound.

There's not any point in even trying to sleep, not with another person in the room. Especially this person. She was practically begging me to flash her earlier. God only knows what she might do if I go to sleep.

Besides, what if I snore? Or drool?

I sit up. Stretch. Make a big show of looking her over. She's digging in a backpack that looks like it's been dragged behind a car. I open my mouth to make some crack about it—but then I remember Coach Kline. I don't want to be in a real class. And I don't want to get benched.

"Look," I tell her, "you leave me alone, and I'll leave you alone."

She ignores me, pulling out an eyeglass case. I notice she's got light-brown freckles sprinkled on her nose and cheekbones. She might look half human if it wasn't for that hair. And those clothes.

She takes out these little half glasses, like something an old-lady librarian would wear. She puts them on, but barely; they look like they're about to fall off the tip of her nose.

But her actual face is kind of delicate-looking. No zits. Yeah, she could be almost decent-looking. Too bad she dresses like a bag lady. With fluorescent hair.

"You probably don't know Coach Kline," I tell her. "He said if there's any trouble in here, he'll kick my ass."

She doesn't say anything.

"He'll kick yours, too," I add. "So don't think you can get away with anything."

"Coach Kline." For just a second she glances up over the rim of her glasses. "Twentysomething, black hair, blue eyes, unshaved look?"

"Yeah."

She's busy again. "In that case," she says, pulling one of her textbooks out of the backpack, "I might go for a little ass-kicking."

If she was a guy, I'd know that was a sexual remark. However, she's not a guy. She's a girl and I'm not sure what she meant. She might be one of those feminists, and want to take on Coach for real. Like arm-wrestle him.

"Whoa," I say. That seems like a good neutral comment.

She flips the book open. It's an English book. She's got the place marked with a piece of notebook paper, torn in half. It's the top half. With writing on it.

Not much. Just a few words on each line, sprinkled down the page. It's upside down, to me.

But I'm staring at that piece of paper, and I can feel the hair standing up on the back of my neck.

"What's *that*?" I point, to show there's no way I'm actually going to touch it.

She's giving me that look again, over her glasses. "It's a poem," she says, in her boy-are-you-stupid voice.

Of course—a goddamn poem. I'd recognize one a mile away. Not just from English class, either. I've seen a ton of them, in Grace's books, in her notebooks, on the margins of her papers. She's practically dripping with them.

But this is not Grace, and I don't have to pretend to be sensitive.

"Jesus," I say in disgust. "A poem. I knew it." I look away and make this big shudder, like "get that thing away from me."

"Jesus," Greenland says, even more disgusted. "A Philistine. I knew it." She makes an even bigger shudder.

We don't even look at each other after that. We've both made our point. Although I don't know what hers is.

She goes back to her book; I lay my head back down on my arms without saying another word. I act like I'm going to sleep, so she doesn't get the urge to tell me *she* wrote the poem. I don't even want to know.

Girl writers. I attract 'em like shit attracts flies.

After sixth-period athletics I go straight home. I pull my car up in the garage, next to the utility room. I get my stuff off the floorboard, then buzz the garage door down while I'm turning off the security system.

This whole day has sucked big-time, on account of I'm not going to get any sleep in assistant anymore—thank you, Greenland!—and on account of I'm a Grace addict who didn't get my fix today.

When I walk in, the house is quiet like always. My sister, Cass, Little Miss Perfect, is still at school.

Mom's at work. She works too much—it's like ever since the divorce she can't get enough money. For a while there, when Dad didn't want to split and Mom did, money was this major issue between them. She'd always slam the phone down when she got through talking to him. And now, even though they get along okay, she still works like somebody's got a gun to her head.

On my way through the family room, I see the cordless

phone. It's right there, on the end table. The answering machine's next to it, with the light blinking—and for a second hope rushes over me. Hope that it might be you-know-who.

"Don't be an asshole," I tell myself, and hit the button and listen to the message. Of course it's not Grace, it's Whorey Dori, this sophomore girl whose last name starts with a *K*, but it's hard to pronounce and I can't remember it. What I *can* remember is that she used to sleep with Jordan Palmer, a senior who plays first base for the baseball team. He's told some really mind-boggling stories about her, and you'd think it'd be a good thing that a certified nympho is leaving me messages, wanting me to call her if I get a chance.

But I know what she wants. All she wants is to talk about Palmer. To ask about him, to find out if he's dating anybody, if he's mentioned her at all, if there's any hint that he might still like her. Palmer is the only subject she knows, he's the only thing she wants to talk about.

And the only subject I know right now is Grace, and talking to anybody who's not her sounds about as fun as making do with a stale potato chip when there's an all-you-can-eat buffet right next door.

So I don't save the message. I erase it, and think how on one hand you've got girls like Grace, who lead this sheltered life and get all shocked when you forget and use the F word in front of them. Then you've got girls like Dori, who give the F word a whole new meaning. From what I hear, anyway.

Still, I'm wishing Grace had been the one to leave a message.

Cass—my sister—gets out at four o'clock. Her bus won't get her here till at least four twenty. There's not going to be anybody around until then.

I could do anything I wanted for the next forty-five minutes. I could call anybody and not be hounded by Cass wanting to use the phone.

Of course, I couldn't call Grace.

"This time *she's* going to call *me*," I tell myself.

And even if I was stupid enough to call her, it would look pretty desperate, the phone ringing right as she walks in the door.

I walk over to the clock. I'm not going to call, of course . . . but if I *did*, four o'clock would be soon enough. Four o'clock would give Grace time to get home. It would give me time to hear the sound of her voice, not get into anything heavy before Cass gets here. Just hear Grace's voice, maybe make her laugh a few times so I'd know I was forgiven.

But it couldn't be exactly at four—if I was going to call, which I'm not. Exactly four o'clock—that'd look too planned. At least five after four. Or six after four, that would look completely unplanned. Yeah, that would be good. If I was going to call, it would be at four oh six.

Right now it's three forty-one.

I go into the kitchen and open the fridge. Take out a Dr Pepper. Pop the top. Drink a little. Stick the can back in the fridge. It'll get flat now, Mom'll gripe, big deal. I was hungry when I came in, but I'm not now. I shut the fridge. What time is it?

Three forty-two.

I decide I'll go to my room. Take off my shoes, maybe. Relax. But on my way through the family room, I see the phone. The phone's right there, on the end table.

It would probably actually be a good thing, to call Grace. She might even be impressed—here I am, a super-sensitive guy, calling to make up for what I did wrong. Whatever that was.

Okay, so I'll call. I'll just give her a few more minutes to get home. I'll wait till three forty-five. No, three forty-six—so it won't look planned. And if she's not home yet, if I get her machine, I'll just hang up.

I sit on the couch next to the phone.

One of the throw pillows is kind of flat. I pick it up and punch it back into shape. Toss it up a few times, catch it. Set it down in my lap.

Okay, I'll just lay the phone right here. Here, on this

pillow. I'll just hold it, till three forty-six.

Right here. Yeah.

Oh, what the hell.

I pick it up and start pushing the buttons.

Then it's ringing, and by the time that first ring's over God himself couldn't pry this phone out of my hand.

"Hello?"

I blank out for a second.

It's her *dad*.

I've met the man several times. I've just never talked to him on the phone. What's he doing home from work? He sounds a lot scarier on the phone.

I'm clutching the pillow now, against my chest. Trying to think.

"Hello?" he says again.

"Uh," I say. "Is Grace there?"

"Who's calling?"

"Uh . . . Colt. I mean Colton. Trammel."

"Well, Colton, I thought that was you. Grace is not home yet."

"Oh," I say. I glance at the clock. It's three forty-three. Too early! I should have waited. Why couldn't I wait? It was only fifteen minutes, or twenty, or whatever.

"Rosalyn," Mr. Garcetti hollers. I wince. "When'll Grace be in?"

"Anytime now." Mrs. Garcetti's voice is faint.

Now I've totally screwed up. I can't call her back. *She* won't call *me* back, for sure. I'll never even know if they told her I called.

"Who is it?" I hear Mrs. Garcetti call.

"Colton Trammel," Mr. Garcetti yells to her.

I've got a corner of the pillow in my mouth now. I'm biting down. Hard.

"Tell him she'll be in anytime now," Mrs. Garcetti calls.

"Colton," Mr. Garcetti says into the phone. "She'll be home anytime now."

I take the pillow out of my mouth. "Oh," I say. "Okay."

There's this silence. Am I supposed to wait, on the phone? Am I supposed to say something? Ask something?

I hang up.

Smooth, that's me.

CHAPTER TWO

Whipped

The next morning I'm not feeling too good.

When I look at myself in the mirror, I can't stand seeing the eyes of a wimp who caved in and tried to call Grace yesterday. Not only tried, but failed.

Pride: 0, Grace: 1.

In the mirror I see one of those guys that apologize when he didn't do anything wrong. Who sits at home when *she* can't go out. Who comes trotting when *she* snaps her fingers.

This morning, when I look in that mirror, I see a guy who's whipped.

Then I tell myself, at least I'm not like Dori. I haven't called people to ask about Grace, the way Dori does about Palmer. At least I haven't done that. Those Trammel balls of steel must still be hanging solid somewhere under there.

Way under there.

Okay, I say to myself, looking in the mirror. I'm going to give myself the old pep talk.

So: Here's the deal, Trammel.

You're a baseball star. You're looking good—nice clothes, by the way! Your friends are the most important people in school. You've got your own transportation, and a good-sized, regular allowance from the old man. You've gone out with some pretty fine-looking girls. Still can, any time you want! Colton Trammel, you are the Man!

My face in the mirror looks tired. I couldn't get a smile on it if I forced the corners of my mouth up with toothpicks and Scotch tape.

All right, I tell the mirror, that's enough. You've got to get this thing under control.

So before I go to school, I do a thing I heard about on TV. I put a rubber band around my wrist, because what I'm going to do is snap it every time I think about Grace. Every thought of Grace will be connected with pain. Negative whadyacallit. It works for smoking and losing weight. It should work for this.

I have to pop the rubber band right when I get in the car, because there's that empty passenger seat, where she always sits.

And again, backing out of the driveway, because I've

got to put my arm around the back of her seat, to turn and look.

And again, when I get to the end of the block, because if I turned right instead of left, I'd be heading toward her house.

I pop my wrist twice more going up the hill that leads past Haley Turner's house, where me and Eric chased a bunch of girls who wrapped my house with toilet paper during a slumber party a couple of years ago. Including you-know-who.

Have you ever noticed the more you try not to think about something, the more you do?

By the time I pull into the parking lot at school, I've popped my wrist twenty-three times.

And while shutting off the engine and unbuckling, I get a whole series of snaps trying not to wonder if she'll be in the front foyer today. How am I supposed to stop thinking about her if she's going to be right there in front of me?

I hang around in the car, acting like I'm digging for something in the glove compartment every time somebody walks by so I don't look like a goof, sitting there all alone. And snapping, too—there's Misty, Grace's good friend. *Snap.* Has Grace told her she's mad at me? *Snap.*

Snap.

Snap.

• • •

My wrist is bright red by the time the bell rings and I go to biology. But I still think maybe there's a chance of getting control of the snapping situation, if I actually try to concentrate on my work for a change.

So I sit there and try to read the stupid busywork assignment Ms. Keller has written on the board. I even look up every word I don't know in the glossary in the back of the book.

Chlorophyll: the green pigment found in the chloroplasts of plant cells.

I knew that already. Didn't I?

Grace would have known it.

Snap.

Greenland glances over. She looks at my rubber band but doesn't say anything.

She'd better not.

She doesn't have to. "Trammel. Pssst. Trammel." I look around; it's Michael McMillan. "What's with the rubber band?" he asks in this stage whisper.

Haley Turner's leaning forward. She wants to hear too.

Greenland's already gone back to her book. She turns another page. It's a relief to know there's somebody who doesn't give a single shit what I do.

"Nothing," I say over my shoulder. I act like I'm reading.

"He's trying to quit smoking," Haley guesses, behind me.

Grace doesn't like smokers. *Snap.*

"Pssst. Trammel," hisses McMillan. "You trying to quit smoking?"

Snap. "I'm trying to *read*," I mutter. McMillan is almost sixteen and his voice hasn't changed yet. But his older sister is a varsity cheerleader, so he gets to hang around on the fringes of the people who count.

No way I'm going to get the whole two pages read before Ms. Keller starts class.

I see Greenland glance at the board and take out a piece of paper. Then I notice the board says to read pages eighty-nine to ninety, then do the questions on page ninety-one. I also notice my wrist is starting to get a little puffy, from the abuse it's taking. From thinking about . . .

Grace.

Snap.

It's to the point where the pain reminds me of what I'm *not* supposed to be thinking about.

Snap.

"I didn't know he smoked," I hear Haley whisper.

I give up reading and take out a sheet of paper. I'll have to hurry and copy the answers off Greenland before she turns hers in.

When I pull my book closer, it knocks my pencil off the table. The pencil hits the floor and rolls to the side. It comes to a stop just on the other side of Greenland's chair.

I try to catch her eye, but she's riffling through her textbook. She's got on those stupid glasses.

"Hey, Greenland. Hand me my pencil, will you?"

She puts her finger on the page to hold her place, turns her head and looks at me over the rim of her glasses.

I point to my pencil, on the floor.

She peers under the table. The pencil's about six inches away from her shoe. She stretches out her leg, gets a toe on the pencil.

She kicks it away. It shoots across the room and disappears under one of the other lab tables.

"Don't call me Greenland," she says. And pulls her paper half under her book—so now I can't get a good look.

"Fuck you," I mutter under my breath.

"No thanks."

I think about whether it's worth getting up and walking across the room to get my pencil. Even if I do, I still won't be able to finish reading the pages and I still won't be able to do the questions myself.

I decide I don't feel like working anymore today. It's

not worth it. I shut my book and lean back in my chair with a sigh. I think about how bad I am at biology. No wonder Grace doesn't want to talk to me.

Grace.

I dig my finger under the rubber band—and then *pop!* Suddenly nothing's there.

The damn thing broke. From overuse, I guess.

Who cares? What difference does it make? I'm snapping as much now as when I put the rubber band on this morning.

Well, what's so bad about being whipped, anyway? So what if my insides are turning to marshmallow? The important thing is that I don't *show* it. Not on the outside, where somebody could see.

I can feel old Greenland—no, *Chlorophyll*, my green-pigmented lab partner—sitting there next to me. She's a girl, like Grace. She's a reader, like Grace. A poem writer, too. This could have been Grace in my class, sharing my lab table. Every sophomore has to take biology. Why'd it have to be Chlorophyll sitting here?

The broken rubber band is on the corner of the lab table. I pick it up by one end. I pull the other end back, taking aim at Alicia Doggett, across the room.

Snap. The rubber band hits her in the back of the head. Alicia gives a little jump, then touches the spot where the rubber band hit and turns to squint around the room.

I'm already leaning on one elbow, looking out the window. I don't even pretend to be interested in biology.

What difference does it make? I'm going to get a zero, after all. No matter what I do.

At lunch I eat with the same guys I always do, Eric Darnell, Patrick Childers, Stu Vernon. We eat in the cafeteria for a change, because Eric and Stu didn't bring enough money to eat off campus. We're going to eat fast, so we can go out and hit some balls—but almost right away these freshman girls come over and sit at the table next to us. They're flirting like crazy, even though as far as I've heard not one of them has ever put out.

Silver Stanton pulls up a chair. I don't know how I feel about it. She's not Grace, but she is a girl, and she *is* pretty hot. She can't help it that she's got the same name as the Lone Ranger's horse. She used to kind of look like a horse too; when she was in fourth grade, and I was in fifth, I used to call her "Hi-yo Silver" and offer her apples from my lunch. But then she got braces that reined in those big teeth, and if I was to walk in off the street today, not knowing any of that, I'd have to say that she looks like a model.

She hangs with the right people. She puts a lot of

money into clothes, and it shows. There's no reason I should be sitting here wishing it was Grace who was smiling just because she's near me. Tossing her hair back over her shoulders.

That's Silver's best feature: her hair. It's straight, shining. Sort of a whitish gold. Like a horse's mane.

But all things considered, Silver has nothing to be ashamed of. Don't ask me why I can't shake the picture of a horse when I look at her. Since her dad paid off the orthodontist, she really is hot. So when she starts pushing herself on me, I don't exactly meet her halfway—but I don't walk away or trade places with Stu, or say I've got to go, either.

"What's today's date?" Silver's asking me.

"I don't know."

"The thirtieth," Eric says.

"Ooh. I've got a couple of movie passes that expire today. Hey, Colt. You want to help me use them up?" She flings her hair back over her shoulder again.

Suddenly I'm fucking irritated. Grace's got hair about the same length, but she doesn't toss it around like she's posing for pictures in the winner's circle.

"I dunno," I tell Silver, although I know I ought to go out with her just to prove to myself that I'm not whipped. "I'm kind of busy."

"Well, if you get unbusy suddenly, give me a call.

Otherwise I'll give them to my brother."

Whatever. I shrug. "Sure. I'll let you know." One of the other girls giggles, and she and Silver exchange meaningful looks. It's pretty junior high, and I'm not in the mood today. I just want to be outside where I can *breathe* and think about something besides Grace.

Baseball.

After eating, Eric, Patrick, Stu, and I go out to the parking lot and get my equipment bag out of my trunk. We walk down to the fields to hit a few in the time we have left.

Me first, of course. I tighten my batting glove just a little, flex my fingers. Get a firm grip on the bat. Toss the ball into the air, and . . . *whap!*

The ball sails toward the left-field fence. Eric takes off, arms and legs pumping, but the ball's faster, and he ends up hunting for it just in front of the fence.

On my first team—the Marlins—my coach always told the other kids, "Keep your eye on the ball! Watch the ball hit the bat!" But he never had to say it to me, even though I was just as little and new as the rest of them.

My coaches have always treated me like I know what I'm doing.

Because I do. Baseball is the only thing that ever came natural to me. Besides lying, that is.

• • •

In fifth-period assistant, there are no papers to grade. I'm not in a great mood, anyway, because I just ate my lunch with a girl who wasn't Grace, and let me tell you, it was about as exciting as helping my mom fold laundry.

Of course I can't sleep, because Chlorophyll the Pencil Kicker is sitting right there reading one of her stupid books. I'd like to show her what happens to chicks who kick Colt Trammel's pencil, but she might tell Miss A. and Miss A. would tell Coach. And Chlorophyll's not worth the concentration it would take to plan some big anonymous revenge that'd really make her miserable.

I decide I'll just mess with her a little.

"Hey, you know, I'm kind of starting to like that hair," I tell her across the table. "I was thinking I could dye my hair green, too. Where do you get yours done?"

She doesn't even look up.

"It reminds me of food," I tell her. "Pickles, okra, broccoli. Hey—maybe I could go for purple. Like grape jelly. Or . . . let's see. What color is pizza?"

Chlorophyll puts her finger on the page, to hold her place. She raises her head to look at me—but she doesn't seem mad. "I was just thinking about you," she says, and she sounds almost friendly. "I happened to be reading this"—she taps her finger on the page—"and it's got *you* written all over it."

I'm not sure what to say. Which doesn't stop me from saying something anyway. "Must be about studly sex machines."

"Listen." Her voice drops almost to a whisper.

> *"And while the sun and moon endure*
> *Luck's a chance, but trouble's sure,*
> *I'd face it as a wise man would,*
> *And train for ill and not for good.*

"I'll skip this next part," she tells me. "It's basically comparing poetry to beer." Which perks my ears up— but she's already going on:

> *"But take it: if the smack is sour,*
> *The better for the embittered hour. . . ."*

She stops suddenly and looks me dead in the eye. "What do you think that means?"

This whole situation's so weird that just for a second I hesitate.

But just for a second.

"It means you're a fucking psycho," I tell her.

"Wrong!" She thumps the open book with her hand.

"It means that you're my vaccination."

"Your vacc—"

"See, Golden Boy, you're a pain in the ass right now, but gradually you'll make me immune to all the other morons in this oppressive caste system you call a school. You're my cowpox, my measles shot, my DPT booster."

I start to say something about at least my hair's not the color of snot, but I'm not really sure what all she just said, and besides, snot comments are too fourth grade.

And she's already bending back over her book. Like she's already immune to me.

I think about what she said. She said I was a pain in the ass. She didn't exactly call me a moron.

Did she?

And it's too late now anyway—to tell her not to call me one. Besides, I don't see how she could have picked up on it. Most people think I'm just lazy.

She keeps her nose in her book. Which is good, because from then till the end of the period, it's as if my tank's run dry. As if what she said put the brakes on any more words coming out of my mouth.

I can't remember the first time I knew I was stupid. It must have been in kindergarten or first grade, when everybody else could already tell the letters apart and I couldn't, even though I started school a year late on account of my birthday's in June and my dad didn't want me to be the smallest boy in my class for the rest of my life. But even with a year's head start, I kept getting the letters mixed up. I still don't read so good.

But I am good at copying, lying, cheating. I get notes like "doesn't work up to potential," and "would rather entertain his classmates than work."

And that's why I could always sit through a whole class period, doing nothing but watching Grace. I'd give anything to be smart like that. The only smart I am is smart-mouthed. And if somebody like Grace—intellectual, pure, refined—could fall for me, then nobody will ever guess that I'm just plain fucking stupid, after all.

Sixth period is athletics. That means different things depending on who's taking it, and the time of year. Most of the guys I know do football in the fall and then basketball or baseball or track in the spring.

For me, it means weight training in the fall and baseball in the spring. Football's okay—I used to play in junior high—but it's not worth fucking up my future with a cracked collarbone or even a broken finger. Jesus, a broken finger! That could ruin everything.

So right now, in the fall, I do weight training. It's me and a few of the other baseball guys that Coach likes, and we don't screw around too much because Coach holds our lives over our heads. If he gets mad, we'll get benched or demoted to second string—or even cut. And I'm the only sophomore on varsity, so Coach could easily send me down to JV.

That's why I'm here every damn day, focused on keeping in shape for the spring. Me, a guy you couldn't count on to show up for his own funeral.

I change clothes and go straight down to the weight room. I'm the first one there. I pick up a thirty-pound dumbbell and take it over to the curl bench. I straddle it and start in on my left arm.

Jordan Palmer and Max Gutterson show up next. They're both seniors, and they're both in baseball. Both played football up till last year, when Palmer sprained his back and his doctor told him he couldn't tackle anymore. Gutterson had one too many concussions.

Palmer is like me in some ways. He lives in the same neighborhood I do, which means he's not hurting for money. He's got a neck like a bull, but eyelashes like a girl—he's a good-looking bastard, like me—but Jordan Palmer never had to work at just getting through the day. His life is smooth as silk; you can bet he's never had a teacher talk to him through her teeth, with veins bulging in her forehead like she's about to have a stroke. He's one of those High Academic people that always have the right words and the right tone of voice with teachers and parents. And even more with girls. He's screwed more times than a Black & Decker power drill.

He nods a hello at me as he takes a seat on the leg-press machine. If I wasn't on varsity, he might not even admit I was here, me being an underclassman.

"I'm telling you, that's bullshit," he says to Gutterson, slipping the key between the plates. "It's because he's still in football and you're not."

"That's what I figured," Gutterson says. "But she says it's because he asked her first."

Gutterson is built like a side of beef; he'd like to pound me just for being a sophomore, but he follows Palmer's lead, and Palmer is too cool to pound.

"She has to say that. Social-climbing bitch." Palmer grips the handles on either side of his seat. "Ready?" he asks Gutterson, who puts both hands on Palmer's knees.

I watch them while I'm counting out twenty reps on my right arm. Palmer braces his feet on the pedals, knees bent, and nods to Gutterson.

"Aaa . . ."

Palmer's neck cords strain—he tries to straighten his legs, to force the pedals out and the heavy plates upward.

"—rrah!" Gutterson drops his own body weight on top of Palmer's knees, forcing Palmer's legs straight. Cables creak. Palmer's face is frozen in a snarl of effort and he's not breathing. His legs are fully extended.

Coach has yelled at them for doing that, but Palmer doesn't care if he breaks both legs and has his kneecaps sticking backward like a chicken for the rest of his life. He just wants to up his leg press.

So here we are, me, a lowly smart-ass of a sophomore, and two eighteen-year-olds with five-o'clock shadows at two o'clock in the afternoon. And they're the ones who need supervision.

"'Kay!" It comes from somewhere behind Palmer's teeth. Gutterson leaps back at the same instant Palmer's legs give out. Cables whir; the weights come crashing down. Palmer's done the one and only rep of his first set.

Now he's got to rest. He wipes his hands on his towel, then swipes his forehead.

"That's the only problem with baseball," Palmer tells Gutterson. "The uniforms. They don't attract the chicks. Not like football uniforms."

"It's those pads," says Gutterson. He leans forward, moves the key down, adding twenty pounds for Palmer's next rep/set, then sits on the bench next to Palmer. "Pads'll make anybody look like Arnold fucking Schwarzenegger."

"Like you'd attract a lot of chicks from the bottom of a dogpile," I mutter to myself.

Not low enough, though. It's a lucky thing Gutterson's too lazy to walk over here. He looks for something to throw at me, but the only thing at hand is Palmer's sweaty towel.

He throws it anyway. I duck, and it only catches me on the shoulder before falling to the floor.

"What do you know about attracting chicks?" Gutterson says.

"Enough." I scoop up Palmer's towel and debate snapping one at Gutterson's crotch just to see him vault into midair. I end up tossing it back to Palmer. I don't feel like getting pounded today.

Palmer drops the towel to the floor. "Trammel, my lad," he says calmly, "the only thing you've ever laid is a fart."

Where the rest of us have to work to get anywhere with a girl, all Palmer has to do is smile in their direction, say a couple sentences, and there they are with their skirts hiked up around their ears. He is hands down the most experienced guy in the school, if you believe what he has to say about it. Which I do. Some of those details nobody could make up.

And I may not have as much experience as Palmer does—nobody could—but he doesn't know that. Besides, I've got balls. Most times, balls are all it takes to make people think that you've got it more together than you really do.

"Hey," I tell Palmer, dead serious, "I've done it ways

you can't even imagine."

"Oh yeah?" Palmer and Gutterson exchange smirks. "Like what?"

I pick my dumbbell up again, and start another set. I'm thinking. "Scuba diving," I tell them.

"Scuba diving?"

"Yeah. Forty feet down."

"You're full of shit, Trammel."

I ignore Gutterson, like I'm focused on my biceps. It works—when I don't argue he glances at Palmer, who's watching me now, thinking. Palmer's probably done the deed in all kinds of weird places. He knows anything is possible.

"Where was this?"

"Bahamas," I say. "Back in August." We did go to the Bahamas, but it was three years ago, when I was thirteen. And I did go scuba diving, but it was with my mom and sister. And we only went to twenty-five, thirty feet.

I switch the weight back to my right hand, and start my last two sets. I can talk, easy, while I'm pumping these light weights—I just can't count while I'm doing it. "It was this girl I met at the hotel. We only did it once, scuba diving. But we'd already done it back in her room a few times."

I keep my voice matter-of-fact, I keep my eyes on the weight, going up, going down. I have no idea how many reps I've done—but I can tell Palmer doesn't know whether to believe me or not.

"Bull." Out of the corner of my eye I see him and Gutterson glance at each other again. "You couldn't get any traction in the water."

I lower the weight to the floor and straighten. Then I smirk at Palmer and shake my head, like he's an idiot. "You don't need traction. You're floating."

Palmer just raises an eyebrow at me, then turns to Gutterson. "Ready?" Gutterson gets up and puts his hands on Palmer's knees again, while Palmer grips the handles. "Aaarrr!" They work together to force Palmer's legs straight; Palmer's shaking and sweating. After a few seconds he nods, and Gutterson jumps back as Palmer's legs turn to jelly. The plates drop with a crash.

Palmer scoops up his towel from the floor, wipes his forehead. "What was her name?" he asks me.

"Twyla."

I don't know where it came from. It's great. It's so weird it's got to be a real name.

"Twyla? What the hell kind of name is that?"

"Dutch. She was on vacation with her parents. They liked to party, so she had a lot of free time. I was the one who had trouble ditching—my mom's into the family vacation thing. She was all 'Now, how do I know this diving trip will be supervised?'" I say that part in a falsetto, then go back to my own voice. "It was supervised plenty . . . on the boat."

At that Palmer's face slides into a grin—he gives me a "way to go" nod—and then doesn't say another word.

I should feel good because I got Palmer and Gutterson to believe this great lie, but *I* know I'm probably the only virgin on varsity. Well, technically, anyway—in some countries I might not be considered a virgin.

When I walk into the house after school, I just stand there, looking down at the phone. Funny how if I just barely even touch a few buttons, *bip-bip-boop-bip*, I could be talking to Grace. Hearing her voice. Just a few little numbers, *bip-bip-boop-bip*.

I find myself picking up the phone. It feels nice in my hand, smooth and rounded, not too heavy, not too light. It's not me pushing the buttons—my fingers are doing it all on their own, very slowly: *bip . . . bip . . . boop*.

It's pleasure and torture at the same time. It's kind of a rush watching my fingers dial Grace's number, wondering how far they're going to go. *Beep . . . bip . . . bip . . .*

No. No way am I going to crawl. I crawled yesterday, and look where it got me. A sore wrist.

Shit. I am in bad shape. There's only one thing to do. I hit the off button.

Then I pull out the school directory, turn the phone back on, and call Silver. Colton Trammel doesn't roll over and beg—not without a fight.

"Hey. This is Colt," I tell Silver when she answers. "Turns out I just got unbusy."

"I heard this is a really good movie," Silver says, as we're walking into the theater a couple of hours later. We traded in the passes for tickets to *Last Kiss*.

Last Kiss is a tearjerker of a chick flick. You can tell by the posters. Silver's walking so close that her hand keeps brushing against mine. Her purse is looped over her shoulder like a saddlebag.

I hadn't really thought about what movie we would see. The point is I'm not lying around crying my heart out just because Grace is mad. But once we're past the ticket taker, I see that there's an R-rated action movie playing on another screen—a movie I've really been wanting to see, whenever it came out.

Well, it's out. So now I've got to act quickly, no arguments. I grab Silver's hand and pull her aside to sneak into a *good* movie.

She doesn't argue. She doesn't let go my hand when we're in the theater, either.

The story takes place on a submarine, and the exciting part is they could all drown any second. Plus there's tons of explosions and fight scenes, and there's also a topless dancer who stowed away to escape the mob, so there's a half-naked woman to look at. It's everything you'd ever want in a movie.

You'd think I'd be happy to see this particular movie with a non-Grace. Silver doesn't seem to mind the half-naked woman thing, whereas Grace always gets offended and says how it's sexist. I don't know what she wants, like they're going to show a bunch of half-naked men running around on a submarine, just to make it equal. Nobody would go see that.

But Silver doesn't say a word about the half-naked woman or the movie. She just sits there watching and popping her gum, and once, when I realize I haven't heard her popping for a while, I glance over and she's looking at me instead of the screen. And when it's over, which is when Grace lists everything she liked and didn't like about the show, Silver just walks out with me and starts talking about how she's got to find a new guy to cut her hair because the old one made her wait an hour last time.

I'm not really listening, but I'm not saying much either. I'm not used to being with a date who doesn't give a shit what we just saw.

"You want to go somewhere?" I hear Silver say.

I shrug. "Like where?"

"Like . . . St. John's?"

I look over. She's smiling at me. No sign of gum being chewed—maybe she threw it away already, getting prepared. Because the dead-end street behind St. John's Presbyterian Church is the prime parking spot for every guy with a car.

Well. Why not? It feels pretty good to have somebody want me more than I want her, for a change. Why not give the chick a thrill? And what Grace doesn't know won't hurt her. It's all her fault anyway for getting mad over a stupid Coke-can ring on her poem and all the other stuff she gets so pissed about.

I drive to the dead end behind the church. Silver's running off at the mouth again, talking about how her dad's going to get her a brand-new Mercedes when she turns sixteen next fall, only he's also going to give her his old Lexus to drive to school because he doesn't want the Mercedes to get banged up.

Finally I get her to shut up by kissing her.

Silver's a pretty good kisser, but tonight she's a little stopped up so we have to pause every once in a while to let her breathe. After a while she lets me touch her up top. She's got nice breasts for a freshman, good sized, but I haven't touched anybody but Grace in a while, and it feels strange, like when you're in a hotel and it's hard to sleep because the bed's not what you're used to.

With Silver, it turns out I can do pretty much whatever I want as long as I stay on the outside of her clothes.

I don't mind too much. She's not Grace, and anyway I don't want to go all that far with somebody who's probably going to go straight home and call the entire freshman class and spread all the gory details about how I performed.

Besides, Silver's nose is starting to make a little whistling sound when she breathes through it.

So after a while I sit back and tell her I've got to get home.

I drop her off at her house—which is huge, one of the biggest ones in the neighborhood—and I'm not feeling too good, because Silver's got her gum back and I know she didn't open a new stick, so she had it hidden somewhere inside her mouth where I couldn't feel it, and I'm kind of grossed out. But mostly I'm thinking how I just got more off Silver Stanton than I got off Grace for the whole first month we dated.

I walk Silver to her front door, say good-bye, don't even bother to try to cop one more feel.

Back in my car I sit there for a second. I've got that feeling, like a volcano, building out of nowhere, about to blow.

It's only a few blocks to Grace's house.

So. I'll just take a little detour—I won't stop, I'll just pass by on the way home. Let off a little of the pressure so the volcano doesn't blow. I'll just look at her house, that's all, and think how she's in there, just a few yards away, doing homework, watching TV.

I drive slowly down her street—that's her house I'm passing now, the one with the winding stone walk, the one with two bay windows.

The volcano's not satisfied.

I turn the car around and drive by again. Slower. Slower.

Well. I'm here, I've taken the time to turn around, she's probably already seen me out the window anyway.

There's no way I can go home without seeing her.

I park in front of her house on the street. Not in the driveway, because that would be like saying I planned to come. Parking on the street means I just happened to be driving by and think of her on a whim. Which is exactly what I did.

I walk up the drive, knock on the door, not too loud. I don't have a clue what I'm going to say to her, but I'll come up with something.

A moment later, Grace opens it.

Let me tell you about Grace. She's got a hot body, although she doesn't act like it. She doesn't throw her hair around and giggle, like some horses—I mean people. She's got hair that's great, it's really truly blond, and soft and straight, and her eyes are a clear green that's so pale it's almost like there's a light behind them, making them glow. And her skin is like—well, I don't know what it's like, but it's clear and white, because Grace doesn't tan, she burns. So she stays out of the sun and her skin is smooth like she's got no pores. Well, that doesn't sound right, but it's true anyway. Grace has never had a zit in her life.

And her attitude is this: She doesn't know how beautiful she is, but she knows about a lot of other stuff. If there's something you wonder about, like why is the sky blue, Grace knows the answer. That's why she has this walk, like I Know Something. She doesn't walk like Silver walks, like Look At Me! Grace is just Grace, and anybody can tell she's comfortable being that way.

And when she opens that door, it's like my head's going to split in half with a smile that I can't stop.

"Who is it?" I hear her mother call.

"It's Colt," Grace calls back. She doesn't *sound* mad. She doesn't roll her eyes or make my name sound like something disgusting.

I did the right thing, coming here.

"We're making candy," Grace tells me, with a glance over her shoulder.

"I just wanted to talk to you for a second."

She just looks at me for a moment, and God! It's been so long since I've been able to look into her eyes, it's like electricity zapping me back to life, even though I didn't know I was dead.

She's got to feel it too; she steps out onto the porch beside me and shuts the door behind her.

Now all I've got to do is not blow it.

"I miss you," I blurt.

Majorly uncool—but it's the honest truth. "Listen. I was wanting to tell you. I really did like that poem. I don't know how it got under my Coke can. I should have put it back in my folder, but I wanted to read it again, so I guess I left it out."

She sighs. "Forget it."

"No, really. I did like it. I liked the metaphor." I don't even miss a beat. *Metaphor* is the one word you need to know if you want to BS about poetry. You don't have to remember what it means. You just have to be able to pronounce it. "I thought you really captured something there." I nod twice, slowly, so I'll look wise. It's my wise nod, and I'm good at it. "Yeah, I thought you pretty much hit the nail on the head. And I really am sorry about the Coke thing—because, you know, I was just about to ask if I could make a copy to keep."

She's frowning down at her feet.

"Hey," I tell her, "I just wanted you to know."

Silence. But she doesn't move to leave. That's good. I want to tell her why else she shouldn't be mad at me, but any other chance at making sense has been sucked into the black hole that is my brain.

"I've been doing some thinking," Grace says, and she looks up at me in that way she has. Which means Buckle In and Prepare for a Serious Discussion. "It wasn't right for me to blame you for getting carried away in the car, when I did the same thing."

I'm not sure what she's talking about—she didn't do much in the car but sit there and breathe heavy when I touched her.

"I'm very attracted to you, physically," Grace tells me. "I think that's why it gets confusing sometimes."

"I get confused too," I tell her quickly. "You're smart, and beautiful, and I get confused, and then I do things without thinking first and that's not good, that's not right. You're just so . . . so . . . I know I'm no Prince Charming—more like the Beast. You know that movie, well maybe you don't, but you're Beauty and I'm the Beast—"

"You're not a beast," she interrupts. "Look. Things were getting kind of passionate. Probably at that moment you really did think you loved me."

I didn't think so—I *did* love her. I *do* love her—but I'm not going to argue about it since she's actually speaking to me.

"But there's something that bothers me," she continues. "It seems like if this was the real thing, we wouldn't have to work at it. It seems like I'd be more . . . swept away. Like we'd just click. A relationship ought to just happen, it ought to be natural and effortless. . . ."

Oh no, I think. And sure enough she's off on the usual, emotional connection and meeting of the minds and *blah blah blah* versus physical attraction *blah blah blah*.

". . . but it's all very confusing, Colt," Grace finishes. "Because I'm really attracted to you. And I miss you when you're not around."

I feel light, like I'm about to float off smiling into the air. She missed me! So what if she says it like it's some math problem she's got to figure out?

"I really do miss you," Grace says softly, almost to herself, and she's got that little line along the inside of one eyebrow that means she's thinking hard, trying to understand. "I guess it's because you help me lighten up; you keep me from thinking too much. From taking things too seriously."

"I don't drain your brain," I tell her, and it's a joke, but inside I feel this sudden pain, like some little guy in there just jabbed me with a tiny knife. Moron!

Grace smiles up at me. "You're good for me, Colt," she says. Like I'm some goddamn vitamin. "And I'm good for you, too, because I get you to think about things you normally wouldn't think about."

"Like poetry," I agree. That almost sounds wise, and I've got to say something so I'll forget the little knife jab.

"There's just something about you. You can be incredibly sweet. And you try so *hard*. Deep down you're very different from the person you try to project. You practically reek of self-confidence—but I can see this scared little boy peeking out."

The thing I wish about Grace is that she'd quit throwing words around all the time. Just once I wish she'd stop talking and just kiss, or get drunk, or laugh like hell.

But I can hear that she's starting to feel sorry for me. So I say "Yeah," real pitiful. Grace has this social worker side, where she likes to fix people. I can't complain—it's the main thing that keeps her from dumping me every time she gets mad.

"The physical stuff . . . it's just happening too fast. Faster than the emotional part. I'm not ready for . . . I think . . ." She takes a deep breath. "I just think we're moving too quickly."

Too quickly? If I went any slower, we'd be going backward!

"What I'd like . . . what I want . . ." Her voice gets so low, I have to lean closer to hear. ". . . is to just back off on some of the physical stuff for a while." She doesn't look super-intelligent right now; she looks shy. "I mean, we can still go out and everything. Just not . . . you know."

"No. I don't know. What do you mean—I can't touch you?"

"I don't mean that. We can kiss and stuff."

"*Stuff?*"

Grace is real big on using the exact perfect dictionary word—except when it comes to sex. Then she doesn't like to even admit people have *parts*.

Grace has always been a little uptight.

"I don't know. I just want to feel more in control."

What? She just said she wanted to be swept away!

Okay, okay. I already knew she's afraid of sex. She's not only afraid of sex, she's afraid because I make her *want* to have sex. And I do make her want to have sex. I know I do.

Okay. Same old same old. She's just innocent, that's all. She's a virgin. So am I. This is good. Isn't it?

Can we take it slower? God!—even slower than we have been? Is that possible? But no, I can do it. Right? I love her. I can't stand being without her. I can do this.

Can't I?

She's looking up at me, waiting. It's my cue.

Even just being with her, I feel like something has loosened. I realize that I'm breathing again, nice and deep. That my breath has been caught in my chest for two days—I can't even breathe right unless I have her.

"We won't do anything you don't want to do," I agree. "You're the boss."

I'm looking down at her, and her eyes are locked onto mine, a little worried, and she doesn't know what to do either, I can tell. God! I want to kiss her. Is that okay? Probably. Is it? Tongues? Maybe. Should I lean in?

"You got new cologne," Grace says into the silence. It's a hint to get closer.

But holy crap! I'm not wearing any cologne.

What she smells is Silver's perfume.

"Um. Thanks," I say, taking a step backward. "It's not really mine. It's a sample. I got it in the mail."

The door opens behind her, and Mrs. Garcetti pokes her head out. "Grace, I need you to stir! Colt?" her mother's head adds. "We're making candy. Want to help?"

"Um, no. No thanks. I've got to go. I've got . . . homework." Mrs. Garcetti smiles. "Can't you—" She breaks off, sniffing. "Uh-oh!" she says, and her head disappears, and as the door shuts again, I smell a funny smell coming from inside, like charcoal and syrup.

"So. I guess I'll see you tomorrow," I tell Grace.

"Tomorrow," Grace echoes. And after another second where I don't know what to do and she's just standing there, she turns and walks back inside.

The glass storm door shuts behind her. Her back is straight, her hair's silk or whatever that shiny stuff is that prom dresses are made of, and it swings a little with each step, brushing the back of her neck. Her rear end sways too, back and forth. Her waist swoops in and then out again, and her jeans are old and soft-looking. They follow every curve and valley, over her hips, down and around and between her legs.

This is how you know when you're really messed up. When the girl you love thinks you're a moron, is afraid of having sex with you, and you still can't stop wanting her.

WEEK TWO

CHAPTER THREE

Balls of Steel

My sister once made cupcakes that looked like breasts.

She didn't notice that they looked like breasts, but boy, did I. Each one had white icing, and a cherry on top. Cass made them for some party she was going to, and she said I couldn't have any.

I wasn't in the mood to fight about it, so I waited till Cass was busy getting ready for her party, and I took a cupcake and ate it. I figured once it was gone, there was nothing she could do about it.

That's what's going to happen with Grace. It's what always happens. I don't fight and argue and toss a bunch of words back and forth about how uptight she is. I just wait till things are getting really hot, and she forgets to worry and *be* uptight. It always works, up to a point. And every time, it works closer and closer *to* the point. One of these days it's going to work beyond the point. That's just the way the world works—you want something bad enough, you eventually get it.

And you know, with Cass and the cupcakes, she never even noticed one was missing. She just grabbed up the tray and ran out the door, and never even looked. Girls are like that—they get all freaked out in advance over something that once it happens, it's going to be in the past anyway. Know what I mean?

One of the few things I've always liked about school is how everybody knows where they fit. You can take one look at somebody and know who they are. You can't get that kind of order anywhere else. Not at the mall, not at the movies—you can't even really count on it at home. Just at school. It's got nothing to do with getting As or understanding poetry, it's got to do with where you belong in everybody else's eyes.

I belong at the top, and everybody knows it. Every day I walk to our spot in the front foyer like I always do, passing all the regular people and the hangers-on. There's a bunch of us who've been in the same crowd since middle school, except for temporary additions like Whorey Dori and a couple of permanent additions who came over from St. Andrew's in the ninth grade already knowing the right people.

The circle's already gathering. Me, and of course Eric

and Patrick, and Preston McGowan's there, and Cara Weston. Morgan, who if you ask me is in PMS mode about ninety-nine percent of the time. Stephanie, who would probably be better for me than Grace, because she's more into partying. I just can't see any point in being attached to Stephanie, though. This summer she dated some kid a year behind us, for cripe's sake.

Looking around, I see that Grace and I are pretty much the top of the top, the cream.

Grace. I step into the circle beside her. She doesn't see me; she's got this look on her face, like she smells something bad.

Right away I know why. It's because McGowan is speaking. Grace, the animal lover, can't stand McGowan ever since one time he told everybody how his kid brother took their hamster for a swim in the toilet, and then accidentally flushed it. That got him on Grace's bad side, and then what really cooked her was that he laughed about it. I *almost* laughed, but just in the nick of time I saw how Grace's eyes were starting to tear up in hamster sympathy. So I wiped that smile off damn quick.

McGowan stops talking, and Grace's face smooths out. She's got her hair hanging down loose today, all straight and shining—no clips, just one side tucked behind her ear, and she's got on some tiny little earring that sparkles, and she's wearing that pale-green blouse that matches her eyes exactly. But she still doesn't see me, because she's waving to someone walking past.

I check to see who it is, because it'd better not be a guy.

It's not. It's a girl. Alicia Doggett, the chihuahua-headed loser.

Grace is a terrific person, but she works a little too hard at being nice, if you ask me. Like waving hello to someone like Alicia Doghead.

Grace has always been that way, never any common sense. It's another of the things we'd always be fighting about, if I didn't keep my mouth shut—the way she has this idea that everybody in the world should be treated equal. Grace has never seen that other people have to be and dress and act a certain way, or else . . . well, they just *do*.

But I don't want to fight. We're back together, so I'm not going to make a deal over it. And it's worth it; when she notices I'm there in the circle, a smile breaks out on her face.

I know that smile. It's the kind you have when you're just so glad to see someone, the happiness has to bust out all over the place.

When I get to biology I have to go by Alicia Doggett on the way to my seat, so I make a little "arf" noise as I walk by. I'm feeling pretty good. I don't bother to see if she cringes or not.

In my seat I look up to the front of the room to see that we've got a substitute—the Fossil.

He's one of the regulars, one of the subs you see in the halls every day of the week. Normally I doze through anything he teaches. The man's about a thousand years old and all his sentences are about a thousand words long. He always comes with a briefcase full of Xeroxed sheets in case the teacher didn't leave a lesson plan. Which Ms. Keller didn't.

I'm having a good morning, and I can't stand ruining it by being bored to death. I'm not tired, I couldn't sleep if the Fossil handed out sleeping pills instead of those goddamn Xeroxes. Even though the only thing I've got to do today is be counted present—which I have been.

I sit there and actually try to work a stupid crossword puzzle, although I really don't want to be in here at all. I need to be doing something physical, not sitting at a lab table where I can't talk or stretch or hardly even move.

It occurs to me that I could easily—easily—make up a story that would make the Fossil give me a pass out of here. At the same time I know I really—really—ought to buckle down and work hard and stop messing around.

In this state they have a no-pass, no-play rule. That means if I don't make at least a C in all my classes the six weeks before the season starts, I don't get to play ball.

So I really—really—need to start taking it more seriously. By the end of December, anyway.

"Mr. Fozzeltini." Haley behind me is waving her hand. "Can I open a window? It's stuffy in here."

It's always stuffy in here. This is one of the old rooms, where the thermostat is set on bake.

The Fossil thinks about it. "Yes," he finally says, and then adds in his usual long-winded way, "I think that would be acceptable."

Haley gets up and opens the window right next to me. In the old rooms the windows slide straight up, not like the newer ones that just push open at an angle.

It looks pretty nice outside, for October. It looks almost summery. Blue, blue skies. Just a few wisps of cloud.

I put my pencil down. The biology classroom is one of two that looks out over the baseball fields. I see—guess who?— Jordan Palmer and Max Gutterson, hitting some balls. Seniors don't have to take a first period if they don't need the credits.

What I wouldn't give to be out there.

A gust of fresh air blows in. It brushes right past the smell of Xeroxed sheets, and lab chemicals, and Formica or formalda or whatever it is that you pickle dead things in.

And then that fresh air touches my nose.

It smells like outside.

I stick my pencil down in the pocket of my folder and shut it. I stack the folder and my book on the table in front of me. I'm ready to think up my lie.

The Fossil's up front, his back to me. He's writing a bunch of letters on the board, under the word *Unscramble*.

While I'm thinking, he mutters to himself. He rubs out a letter with his fingertip and writes another. I hear the scratching of pencils all around.

That's when it hits me.

Why lie? This old guy isn't going to notice if I'm here or not.

The window's partly open. Beyond lie the baseball fields of R. A. Pleasence High School.

It'll be great. It'll be funny. It'll add to the Trammel mystique.

I shove my book and folder onto the wire shelf under my chair. I stand up and step to the window, nice and casual. I open it all the way, like I'm feeling a little stuffy, too.

Nobody says anything.

I check Haley, behind me, in case she's going to complain how it's too windy now.

Haley's frowning down at her paper.

I check the front. The Fossil's still got his back to me.

I turn, still casual, like I'm just leaning against the sill. Now I can see the whole class. My heart's beating a mile a minute.

Michael McMillan raises his head and sees me standing there. He starts to say something.

I give him a warning look. A keep-your-mouth-shut look.

McMillan knows something's up. He leans back in his chair, grinning, ready for the show.

Haley looks up as I turn to lift one leg onto the sill. She gasps and darts a glance over at the Fossil. But she doesn't say a word.

I lift the other leg onto the sill.

Taptaptap. I freeze. It's Chlorophyll, tapping her pencil against the tabletop.

I forgot about her.

She hasn't seen me yet. She's just thinking. She scribbles a word on her crossword puzzle without looking up.

I ease both legs outside. Almost there. But I can't resist—one last look around, legs hanging out the window—to savor the moment.

Half the class is watching me now. Across the room Alicia Doghead is outright gaping. McMillan's nodding in approval. Haley looks scared.

Chlorophyll notices all the heads turning. She looks over and sees me, too. Her pencil freezes over her crossword puzzle.

We're looking right into each other's eyes. Hers are light brown, under dark lashes. Her mouth is kind of small without even a hint of gloss or color—but it's not tattling on me yet. There's no telling what she's thinking. No telling what she's going to do.

I can't help it—I smile at her. A real smile, a genuine Colt Trammel smile. It's the adrenaline, it's the rush from not knowing what's going to happen next.

Her eyes widen, like I just popped a flashbulb in her face.

I couldn't surprise her by almost exposing myself. But a smile—that surprises her.

Which gives me the most satisfaction yet today.

The Fossil drops the chalk back into the chalk tray. "All right," he says, dusting off his hands as he starts to turn around.

A little kick, a little push—and I'm already gone.

It occurs to me on the way to my car that my book and folder are probably going to get stolen out from under my biology chair. Along with my only pencil.

Oh, well. I can borrow today. And buy new stuff tomorrow.

Nobody catches me getting my equipment bag out of my trunk. Nobody catches me going down to the field. And it looks like nobody from my class has pointed me out to the Fossil, even though the field is in full sight of every window.

Palmer just laughs when I tell him I jumped out the window. "Bet old Fozzeltini didn't even notice" is the only thing he says. He and Gutterson let me take a couple of turns hitting. God, it always feels good to get my hands on a bat! When I send one sailing over the fence, I turn and wave at McMillan and Haley, in case they're watching. I even give an extra little wave for Chlorophyll—who might or might not tell.

I don't get called down to the office at all the next period. By lunchtime, I know I'm safe.

Fifth-period assistant, I've already got my head down when I hear the door open and the sound of Chlorophyll's squeaking shoes. Her chair screeches back. Every day it's the same thing—I can tell exactly what she's doing, without even raising my head.

But this time there's something different. A swish and a thud—something lands on the table right by my ear.

I look up. It's my biology stuff.

Chlorophyll sits down without a word.

I pick up the folder. I can see the lump my pencil

makes, down in the pocket.

"Thanks," I tell her, sliding the book and folder to one side.

"You're welcome," she says.

I put my head back down. I'm not sleeping, just resting my eyes. Although I could sleep if I wanted. Because now I know the score—she's a loserette, but she knows when to keep her mouth shut.

For some reason it makes me think about Grace. How it's a good thing that she didn't see me going out the window.

The truth is, Grace and I are not all that much alike. She's bored by baseball, she doesn't drink, doesn't party. I don't understand half of what she says, and I'm pretty sure that if she knew how little I understood, she'd dump me like a used TV-dinner tray. No "emotional connection" and all that.

But it's still going to work. Us, I mean. No matter how unalike we are. I can make it work. That's how bad I want her.

And really, there's good things about us being so different. For one thing, I can really appreciate her. All the bad stuff about me means that I'm the one guy who can appreciate how smart, how deep she is.

And hey, only for a girl like Grace would a guy like me try to be a better person than I really am.

What they say about how opposites attract is absolutely true. Grace and I are opposite, but we're perfect for each other.

I raise my head up, rest my chin on my arms. Chlorophyll's taking out a book like she always does. And those glasses. I'm not saying anything, she's not saying anything. Just like always. But I guess I do appreciate the pencil thing, and I'd like to say something to let her know that was pretty cool.

"Opposites attract," I blurt. I don't know why. It's what I happened to be thinking, so that's what came out.

Chlorophyll opens her book without looking up.

Then I get this dim idea that maybe it sounded like I was saying something about her and me, which I wasn't—Jesus, no way! But of course it came out all wrong. As usual.

But then I realize it doesn't matter that I screwed up. Chlorophyll didn't hear a word I said. She's got her nose in her book.

I guess the vaccination's already working.

I relax and put my head back down.

And from then till the end of the period, all I hear is the sound of a page being turned every once in a while.

After school I bug Grace to call her dad at work and get him to give us the okay to go out for ice cream. I promise to have her home before he gets off work. It's so all-American, he can't refuse. And he doesn't.

So I take Grace to the Marble Slab. Me personally, I don't like having my ice cream slapped around by some technical-school dropout with zits and glasses like the big end of a telescope. But I do like to watch Grace standing there almost breathing on the glass while she watches the guy mix Hershey's Kisses into her double Dutch chocolate fudge. She gets so happy over little things. I could buy her a Porsche, and she wouldn't be as excited as she gets about a crummy little dip of ice cream.

She's standing there, and I'm standing right next to her, and suddenly it's the best afternoon of my life.

I get a Dr Pepper and we sit down. I'm sipping my drink, but mainly I'm busy not saying much because Grace and I get along a lot better when I keep my mouth shut.

"Did you see that new guy at school today?" Grace asks between bites. "The one who's visually challenged?"

"No," I tell her. I watch her take another dainty little bite off her spoon. She'll eventually polish off the whole thing, I know, but you would never guess it to look at her.

"Have you ever wondered what it would be like?"

"What?"

"Being visually challenged."

I think fast. I don't know what visually challenged is. So I've got to decide, quick—which answer is better, yes or no? "Yes" will sound more sensitive, but "no" is the truth and I won't have to back it up with facts.

"Yes," I try. Going for sensitive.

"Really?" She sounds surprised. "What do you think it would be like?"

Shit. "I dunno." Jesus, what should I say? "Bad," I finally guess. And then, when she just takes another bite of ice cream, I give my slow wise nod—twice—and add, "I think it would be really bad."

"I think the whole world would seem different." Grace's drifting into analyze mode. "I think you'd perceive things as three-dimensional, as existing in space rather than as something you just look at. I mean, just sitting here, the world out there"—she gestures toward the other tables, the counter, the pimply-faced guy— "could be two-dimensional, as far as we know, until we touch it. It could be a picture, or a film."

I stir my straw in my Dr Pepper. I nod my head, but I'm thinking about how today Jordan Palmer was telling Gutterson that he and this girl videotaped themselves doing it.

"How can you be sure that something really exists unless you touch it?"

But then, I'm figuring, if I were Palmer, I'd have brought the tape in to show Gutterson. Only Palmer said he'd promised the girl he wouldn't. Which means maybe he was lying about the tape in the first place.

Strange thought, that Palmer could lie the way I do. Probably not as much, though. Nobody could lie as much as I do.

"It could be that blind people actually have greater perception than the rest of us."

I focus on Grace again. Blind people—that's what this was all about. Good thing I said "bad." Jesus, can you imagine if I'd said "good"?

And it's a good thing Grace doesn't have a clue what all goes on inside my brain. Nobody has a clue. I'm not even sure most of the time. It's like the Indy 500 with bumper cars in there.

Grace's face is still and stern right now, but not because of me—it's because she's still trying to figure out this idea about blind people. She's so intense all the time, always, about everything.

Her left eyebrow's drawn in a little, the way it gets when she's chasing down some thought. I can see that tiny little line next to the inside part of her eyebrow. I call it her thinking line.

"God, you're beautiful," I burst out.

The thinking line disappears. Grace looks startled for a second, almost like she'd forgotten I was here. Then her face softens, and suddenly nobody's smart and nobody's stupid. It's Colt and Grace, on the same playing field.

For once she doesn't gripe about me saying "God" like that. Instead she smiles, like I've given her a present. And then, when I don't say anything else, she asks, "Want a taste?"

I'm not really into ice cream, but she's holding the spoon out across the table—she's offering to feed me herself. So I nod, and she does it, she leans forward and lifts the spoon to my mouth. I take it between my lips and my teeth, and then she pulls it out slowly while I'm sucking off the ice cream. Her little thinking line is definitely gone. And she's watching my mouth the whole time.

"Colt." Grace says my name like nobody else can. It sounds like something that tastes good when she says it. "You're really a sweet person." She says it softly, looking at me very intent, the way I guess an artist might, if she was trying to draw the lines of my face. "You've just got this bad-boy façade."

I'm not sure whether to do my wise nod. I'm not sure if "façade" is something I ought to be nodding about.

"Sometimes it's hard to tell who you really are. You're such an enigma."

"Think so?" I ask, like I know what she just said. Forget Word of the Day. Her brain's deep into let's-analyze-Colt mode, so deep that she's forgotten to worry as her body gets totally hot for me.

We're gazing into each other's eyes just like in one of those movies she likes, until Grace realizes that her body's hot for me—you can see the moment it hits her, because her cheeks suddenly turn pink and she ducks her head again and won't look at me for a few minutes.

I think then what I've thought many, many times since Grace and I started going out. She's innocent. And I love her, so I've got to take it slow.

But someday soon, the heat from me and Grace Garcetti is going to melt every drop of ice cream within ten miles.

CHAPTER FOUR

The Suckometer Bottoms Out

So I'm feeling okay again, my life is good, I've got Grace again, and I'm one happy guy . . . until a few nights later, when the shit hits the fan, and suddenly my whole life sucks again.

"No way," I yell. "No way I'm going to let a eighth-grader help me with my homework."

Mom's in my bedroom doorway. Cass is behind her.

"Did you think I sign your progress cards without reading them?" Mom starts counting off on her fingers. "Biology—seventy-five. Geometry—seventy-two. English—sixty-eight." Her voice goes up on the "sixty-eight." "And now you're asking me how to find the area of a rectangle? Colt, at this point you need any help you can get."

"No, I don't." I shoot Cass a "piss off" look. "That last English test was hard. Nobody did good. He said he was going to curve it." Which might be true, Hammond might have said that, I just might not have heard him. "And then he didn't. And this . . ." I bend over my geometry book again. "I can figure it out myself. I just didn't want to take the time."

I don't look up. A couple of seconds tick by. Will Mom buy it?

"What about a tutor?" she asks.

"Don't need one," I tell her. "I can handle it." No way I'm going to sit around with somebody who gets paid to find out how ignorant I am. And who—God!—reports on me to my mom every day!

No fucking way.

"All right," I hear her say. I can breathe again. "But there's a pattern developing here. Every year you put less and less time into your schoolwork. Every semester your grades slide just a little bit lower. A sixty-eight's not going to cut it, Colt. You're perfectly capable of passing. Tell me what I can do to help you. What do you need?"

"I need peace and quiet," I tell her. "So go away."

"Fine. Then I'll tell you what I'm going to do to help you. I'm going make you a promise."

A promise?

"I promise you that if you fail even one class this six weeks, you won't be playing baseball in the spring."

It takes a moment for her words to sink in. "What?" I can't even yell—I'm so mad, it takes another moment for my voice to get up to full volume. "What's that going to do? How's that going to help?"

"Don't yell at me," Mom warns. Cass just stands there, acting like she's real interested in the wall while she soaks all this in, the little leech.

"What's it supposed to do?" I yell anyway. I don't have the words to tell Mom how awful, how more than awful it would make my life, to take away the only thing I'm really good at.

"It'll give you a wake-up call, Colt," she tells me. "There's more to life than sports."

"I almost failed English last spring, too—remember? And I passed, didn't I? I pulled it out. You just don't trust me," I tell her.

"You barely passed. When I had that little discussion with Coach Kline, you managed to summon the energy to pass. You're just going to apply that energy a little earlier this time, that's all."

I cheat better under pressure, I want to tell her. But of course I don't say that. "The state of Texas says I get to play if I pass the three weeks before the season. I've got till the end of December—and that's just to attend practice. To actually play, the state of Texas gives me till the middle of February." Don't ask me how come I can't remember how to find the area of a rectangle, but I remember state law like I'm a lawyer.

"The state of Texas isn't your mother."

"I have no reason to pass if I don't get to play. That's the law, isn't it? No pass, no play. See, I know my history."

"Colt." Mom's got that . . . Mom look. No way Dad would ever say what comes out of her mouth next. "Baseball is a game. I know you like it. I know you do well. I'm very proud of how talented you are. But it's just a *game*."

I'll go live with Dad then, I want to say. But I know Dad won't take me. Not that we don't get along, it's just that he travels a lot. He loves me and all—he's just not much of a family guy, Dad isn't.

"Baseball is what's going to get me into college," I remind her.

"What if you get injured?"

"I won't."

"But what if . . ." Mom sighs. "I refuse to get sucked into this discussion. I'm telling you—balance your interests. Balance baseball with your schoolwork. If you can't manage to keep it all under control, then I'll balance it for you. That's the way it's going to be. Not another word," she adds, as I open my mouth. "Not. One. More. Word."

I can tell she means it because she's talking through her teeth.

I slam my book shut. I wait till she leaves the room, and that little vulture Cass goes with her.

Then I throw the stupid book against the wall.

I'm not going to bother to tell Coach what my mom said—I don't need somebody else on my ass. I know I can work this out. Geometry's not really that hard, it's just the word problems. And there's not all that many of those. I'm pretty sure I can pull a C if I don't even *do* the word problems. And a C is what I need to pass in the state of Texas. Even Mom can't change that.

Biology—well, I've got somebody at my table, now. Somebody smart. I ought to be able to get enough off Chlorophyll to pass biology. If not, Stu's got biology second period. He's not an A+ student or anything, but he'll share his homework for me to copy, and his notes for me to make cheat sheets.

English is the problem. Mr. Hammond doesn't mess with fill-in-the-blank. Never heard of multiple choice. Strictly an essay man, all the way.

In my book there's something wrong when it takes you longer to do a test than it took the teacher to make the test up in the first place.

Looks like I'm not going to be sleeping anymore in

assistant. Looks like I ought to use that time to start figuring out what I need to smuggle in to help me on those extra-long Hammond-style tests.

Looks like there's going to be two of us reading in assistant, from now on.

The next morning in biology Haley Turner's telling me how Silver Stanton thinks I'm cute. Hi-yo! Tell me something I don't know. "She told me to tell you that your answering machine's not working," Haley adds. "She's been trying to get you to call her."

The only thing wrong with my answering machine is that I have to push a button to get rid of Silver's messages. It doesn't automatically erase them for me.

I ignore Haley. While she's taking the hint, I happen to glance at Chlorophyll. She hasn't even looked in my direction, of course. She must have finished up reading her biology, which I should be starting, because she pulls a different, thin book out of her stack. As she starts reading it, twisting a strand of that half-green hair, one of the other books in her stack catches my eye. It's a junior English book.

But she's in sophomore biology, with me.

The wheels start turning.

"Hey, Chlorophyll," I whisper.

She doesn't hear me.

"Hey." She still doesn't know I'm talking to her.

Finally I give her elbow a nudge.

She looks over, startled. She's got that blank-eyed look, the same one Grace has when we walk out of one of those movies where they talk about relationships for the whole hour and a half.

"You a sophomore?" I ask.

She nods.

"You got third period, Mrs. Muldrew?"

"Yeah."

"Accelerated English?" I ask, to make sure.

She's getting her brain back in gear. "You got a point?"

I'm thinking she's already had everything I'm about to be tested on. That's what Accelerated English means; it means they're all a year ahead of the rest of us.

Grace, she's in that class too, but no way do I want Grace seeing how bad I am at something she's great in.

"No." I open my biology book too. "No point." I pretend to read some of the page, because I've got to play this very cool. It takes delicate timing and a perfect hand, to use somebody to cheat off without having them think they got the right to come up and talk to you in the hall.

She settles back into her book. I watch her out of the corner of my eye. I'm thinking. I'm not sure yet exactly what I need her to do.

For the first time, I notice a ring on her left hand. It's

gold, delicate little golden swirls around this milky-colored stone. Doesn't look like anything she'd pick out—I figured her for the skull-and-crossbones type. This looks nice. It looks like a present.

"So, Chlo—Corinne," I say. I've got to start remembering her name. "You got a boyfriend?"

"Yeah." She doesn't look up.

"He go to school?"

"TMU."

Whoa. "A college man," I say. "You two serious?"

"Uh-huh."

I wonder what her boyfriend's like, if they've had sex. Looking at her, I'd say yes. I don't know why, but I'd say definitely yes. Although I'd freak if I had to look down at the moment of passion and see that multicolored shit on her head.

Suddenly I'm curious. "What's he think about your hair?" I ask.

She doesn't answer. She's off in that la-la land book people go to.

So I take a minute to try to reason things out. The main problem is how the hell I'm going to pass Hammond's essay exams. The reality is that I need a comprehensive cheat sheet.

I look over again at Chlorophyll, who already knows everything *I* need to copy down. She's one of the few people in here who's already through reading the biology assignment. She's fast. Fast and smart.

"Hey—" I start, but her real name goes right out of my head. "Hey . . . Chlo."

Shit. I wait, to see what she's going to do.

"What," she says, not looking up.

"Um," I say. "How long you and your boyfriend been going out?" Lame, lame, lame.

She still doesn't look up. "Little over a year."

"No kidding. That's a long time," I tell her. I nod, even though she's not looking at me.

"I got a girlfriend," I mention, when it looks like the conversation's on the verge of being dead in the water.

She doesn't seem overwhelmed by that information.

"Hey, Chlo," I say casually. "You save any of your tests or anything from English last year?"

"No," she says to the book.

"Oh. I thought maybe you were the saving type."

"No."

I'm sunk now.

She flips over a page. "You having trouble in English, Terrell?"

"Trammel," I tell her. I can hear McMillan talking real loud to Haley, so I know they're not listening. "A little," I admit, keeping my voice low.

She just nods.

"Got any advice?" I ask, just in case she's got some kind of good-grades secret I should know.

"Study."

"Oh, thanks." I open my biology book and try to read too. I'm going to ignore her for the rest of the period. She's so fucking helpful. Study.

"Clear your desks," Ms. Keller calls from the front of the room.

Clear your desks? I look up. She's holding a stack of papers.

"All you need is a pen or pencil." She starts passing out the papers.

Holy shit.

"A test?" My voice almost cracks. "You never said anything about a test today."

Ms. Keller doesn't even stop passing them out; she just gives me the eye. "I announced it Friday. And it's been written on the board for over a week. Apparently you haven't been paying attention."

I pick up my biology book and slam it down.

That stops her. She pauses in the middle of the aisle to give me one look. It's a warning look that's supposed to be aimed at me, but it's so intense that the whole class gets quiet.

Then she gets back to business.

The test is short, one page. It's a front-and-back view of

a human body with the skin stripped off. All the muscles have blanks beside them.

I swear she didn't tell us we were having a test. And all I can remember is that the answers are supposed to be long, doctor-type words. Words that I can't even pronounce.

Thank God for Chlorophyll.

I write my name at the top and look over at Chlorophyll's test. She's writing fast, like she knows the answers. She's got her hand over her paper.

I wait, but she doesn't move it.

I try to see over the shoulders of the people in front of me. No go. The blanks are too small, everybody's writing small; I can't see that far.

"Everyone needs to keep his eyes on his own paper," calls Ms. Keller from her desk.

I act like I'm working for a few minutes. Till Ms. Keller gets busy with something else.

"Psst," I hiss in Chlorophyll's direction. When she looks over I make a big show of moving my own hand off my own paper. So she'll get the idea.

But she just raises one eyebrow. Her hand stays right where it is.

I move my hand again, in case she didn't understand. On the paper. Off the paper.

"No," mouths Chlorophyll, glaring now.

I knew it. "Bite me," I mouth back.

She ignores me and goes back to her test. Her covered-up test.

Great. I'm screwed. I do *not* know this. Nobody knows this, except biology teachers. And Chlorophyll.

I eye the test again. I'm trying to remember anything, just one muscle, even. Surely one thing stuck in my head from class. Just one thing—how can I not remember even one thing?

And then it comes. The one thing.

Gluteus maximus. The butt.

Maybe I remember because it's funny. For whatever reason, there it is, in my head. Gluteus maximus.

I start to write it down. Out of the whole stinking morning, this is what I'll have to show. Two stinking words.

I'm trying to sound it out so I don't get counted off for spelling, and I'm saying it to myself: Gluteus, gluteus, gluteus. It sounds familiar.

And then I know why. That's what Coach says, sometimes when he's on the way through the weight room when you've been doing squats or lunges. He walks by and shouts, "Those glutes burning yet?"

What he means is your butt muscles. Glutes.

It dawns on me—I *do* know this stuff. I do! I use this stuff, every day, in the weight room. I know more than anybody else in this room, because I feel the burn in these exact muscles. I work these muscles to the point of jelly every day—upper body on Mondays, Wednesdays, and Fridays, lower body on Tuesdays and Thursdays.

So I'm thinking, what else does Coach say?

Quads. He says that when I'm on the leg press machine. And what hurts like hell, on the leg press machine?

The front of my thighs.

I write *quads* down in the blank. It's not a doctor word. It's just what I know.

I go over the test thinking, what Coach-type exercise makes *this* muscle hurt? And what's he hollering while I'm sweating and shaking?

Lats. Delts. Pecs. Abs. Biceps. Triceps. Traps.

I write it all down. I finish early, of course. I turn in my test while old Chlorophyll's still chewing her eraser, trying to think.

For the first time in—actually, for the first time *ever* in a class, I feel proud.

And for the first time ever, I can hardly wait to get a test back.

I've got no worries now. I'm on a roll. I don't need help. When Mr. Hammond gives us a pop quiz in English, I don't even blink, though I've never heard

Coach hollering anything about Coleridge, this poet who I remember looked like a pop-eyed wuss in the picture in the textbook. Old Coleridge looked like somebody who got the shit beat out of him a lot.

I copy bits of other people's work. I make the sentences as long as possible, and use the biggest words I can think of. Hammond'll love it. Of course he will.

By fifth-period assistant I'm getting a little tired of doing the brainiac thing, but I continue as planned. I open up my English book, because from now on I'm going to by God figure out what it is I'm supposed to *know*. And then I'm going to write it down. And then later I'll condense it down to something I can hide in my palm, or my sock.

The homework is reading something called "A Red, Red Rose." Mr. Hammond said it was by Bobby Burns, like he knows the guy personally. But now I see that can't be possible, because the book says Robert Burns died years and years ago. So I figure it's one of those intelligent-type jokes that I never get.

I don't get the poem, either.

First of all, even *I* can see the words are all spelled wrong. What gives? For ten years the system grades me down for bad spelling, and now they're making me read this shit that looks like pig latin.

Second of all, it's got to be the stupidest thing I've

ever read. Or tried to read, anyway. All *O*s and *my dears*. Did Hammond explain this in class? "The seas gang dry, my dear." What the hell is that supposed to mean?

I shut the book and sit up. I don't need this hassle. I don't need this stress. All I need to pass a test is the Trammel balls of steel—plus a sprinkling of words like *theme* and *meter*.

The trash can is in the corner. I wrap my fingers around one corner of the book and draw my arm back, like I'm going to throw a boomerang, or a knife.

Ka-thunk! A direct hit. The trash can shakes but doesn't fall over.

I know I'll have to dig the book out eventually if I don't want to have to pay for it. The point is I feel better now.

I'm ignoring Chlorophyll, the way she always ignores me. I walk over to the window and hop up to sit on the cabinet underneath, like it's a window seat.

Chlorophyll's deep into her book. She wouldn't notice or care if I fell out the window.

Which is great. I'm free to think my own thoughts, looking out this second-story window at the grass down below, and the asphalt, and the classrooms beyond, in the other wing.

I sit sideways on the cabinet, leaning back against the

windowsill, my legs stretched out in front of me.

I think about last Fourth of July.

Because that was our first real date. Grace's dad said she could start dating when she turned fifteen. Her birthday was on the third, and she spent it with her family. On the fourth I came to pick her up in my car. She had on a white tank top and denim shorts, and her legs just about begged a hand to run up them, they were so smooth. For the first time she slid into the car beside me and it was just us, no Eric or Stu or anybody else from the group. Her hair was tied back, and when she looked at me, her eyes seemed clear green because of the white shirt, I guess. And when she looked straight ahead, her profile was like one of those pieces of jewelry, you know, one of those little round white-and-brown things carved with a woman's face.

I took Grace to see the fireworks downtown. We didn't go to any of the parks or along the river, because we would have been stuck in traffic for hours. Instead I pulled off on this road that I've used in the past for parking. With Grace, though, I brought a blanket and we walked out into the dark field and I spread the blanket so we could sit.

It was breezy, and not hot at all, since the sun had gone down. It was perfect. I didn't talk on purpose, because I didn't want to make an ass out of myself. We just sat together, and she kicked off her sandals, and somehow in the middle of the fireworks show she let me pull her into my lap, and after a few moments her head leaned back against my chest. And when the fireworks were over, we didn't move, just stayed there and kissed for a long time. I didn't try anything at all, and she didn't get mad at me at all, and it was the best night I ever had. In the morning I could still feel the way her arms slid around my neck and how she kissed me back. And the next time I came to take her out, when she saw me coming up her sidewalk, she opened the door to meet me on the porch. And she smiled at me like she'd just gotten a present.

The bell rings. I don't want to move out of the sun, but I know I have to.

I turn my head, and that's when I see Chlorophyll watching me. She hasn't made a move to gather her stuff. Her book's still open. She's just sitting there with her chin on her hand studying me like I'm a plant cell or a para-whatdyacallit, that you look at under the micro-scope and it's shaped like a shoe.

I feel my face getting red. I swing my legs around and jump off the cabinet. She's still sitting there—she doesn't bother to look away, like she doesn't even care if I caught her staring at me.

"Take a picture, Chlorophyll," I tell her as I walk out the door. "It'll last longer."

On the way home I've got Grace on the brain. Thinking about all the making out we did on the Fourth of July—man, I need a Grace fix.

I've been Super Gentleman the past week. In seven days I've worked my way up from hand holding to kissing, being very careful not to piss her off.

I don't want to piss her off. I just want to be with her.

I'm going to call her the second I get in. But when I walk in the door, the phone's already ringing.

I knew it! Grace could feel me thinking about her. She misses me, too! There's a direct line from my heart to hers.

I feel a smile taking over my face as I pick up the phone—it's fate, it's destiny.

No, it's Whorey Dori. The one with Jordan Palmer on the brain.

"Hi!" she says, bright and perky. "Whatcha doing?"

One sinking second later, I tell her, "Not much." Because it's Grace I want to talk to, not Dori, and I know this girl will talk forever.

"What are *you* doing?" I ask.

"Picking out wallpaper."

"Wallpaper," I echo.

"I'm redecorating my room," she says, like that's a really interesting activity. Which it isn't. Not at all. "But I can't decide on a pattern. I need a man's opinion—which do you like better, vines or shells?"

"I dunno," I say. I'm thinking how I ought to hang up, just hang up, Colt! Or say I've got to go and *then* hang up.

I always think that, but I never can seem to quite cut her loose. Probably because she really is pretty fine-looking, for a nobody. And according to Palmer, she'll do anything you want her to, any place, any time.

Now you've got to understand that I'm in love with Grace. No question about it. Always have been, always will be.

But hey, for real, I'm perfectly normal. I'm a teenaged male, I'm supposed to be horny for girls I don't particularly know or like. At least I'm no Palmer, who was once boffing two girls, best friends, and neither knew about the other.

So it's not my fault that just the sound of Dori's voice gives me that feeling, sort of guilty and excited at the same time, like when you pick up a dirty magazine off the rack and you're looking at the pictures, and you're acting like you don't care if anybody sees you, but at the same time you're hoping nobody does.

"I like the shells," Dori's saying, "but I also like the vines because they have these little flowers all around. Flowers are pretty, don't you think?"

"Yeah," I say. "Flowers are nice." I've never mentioned to Grace that Whorey Dori calls me sometimes. Grace might not see it the right way.

"So I'm kind of leaning toward the vines," Dori's saying. "I'll feel like I'm in a forest when I walk in. Don't you think?"

"Yeah, sure," I tell her. "Vines it is."

"How many rolls do you think would it take to paper my room?" Dori's asking.

"I don't know," I tell her. I've never been in her room. I've never been in her house. I don't even know where she lives.

"How much do you think a roll of wallpaper costs?"

"I have no idea." I'm thinking how things start to happen—like one day you accidentally make eye contact with somebody who's not in your group—and then suddenly everything's out of your control and months later here you are stuck sitting around listening to some slut talk about wallpaper and you can't even hang up.

Finally Dori gets down to it, down to the subject she really called about. Just like she always does. "So," she asks, breathless all of a sudden, "you talked to Jordan lately?"

"Yeah," I tell her. "Just saw him in sixth."

I guess I have to admit I feel kind of sorry for Dori. Being in love with this guy who's completely forgotten she even exists.

Still, I make one last try. I tell myself I'm a sap, an ass, that I can't sit here and listen to this girl, that she's a nobody. I remind myself that it's not my problem that she's in love with a guy who used her, then dumped her forever. I remind myself that I'm never even going to be in the same room with her, much less get close and private enough to sample the goods. I remind myself I am not going to get one single thing out of this conversation but lost time.

I tell myself it's time to reach down deep for those balls of steel and tell this loserette to take a hike.

"I guess he's doing okay?" Dori asks.

It's just so fucking sad.

What's saddest of all is that all the stuff she asks about that asshole Palmer is the same stuff I always want to know about when Grace is out of my life.

I know how Dori feels. I don't like this girl, don't need her, don't want anything to do with her—but I know how she feels. And I'd pour melted lead down my own throat before I'd talk to her in the halls, but I'm also not going to be the one to tell her that the guy she loves is out doing a million other girls, every one of which he forgets—just the way he's forgotten her.

So I settle in—just for today, just one more time—for what I know is going to be a long, boring, one-sided conversation. Next time I'll tell her to take a hike. But today I tell Dori, "Yeah, Jordan's doing fine."

WEEK THREE

CHAPTER FIVE

Cold, Cold Paws

Waiting is not one of my strong points.

It's been two weeks since I agreed to let Grace be the boss of our sex life. The Super Gentleman thing is already getting old. I open doors, pull out chairs, and nod wisely. I don't take her parking, and I only kiss her when I'm saying good-bye.

I also keep my hands off her. No joke—we've been out twice, and both times I did some strumming on my old banjo, if you catch my drift, at home before I left to pick her up. That way I wasn't—well, pawing at her is what she calls it.

Don't ask me why it's making love when it's in a movie, and it's pawing when it's just us in a car.

God, I'd take either one.

Another thing I'm having to wait for is the stupid test grades from biology and English. Now, I understand

Mr. Hammond insists on writing little notes on everybody's paper. I don't mind waiting for that, because it'll be nice to get a bunch of good comments in red ink for a change.

But Ms. Keller is just plain lazy. She's sitting on her ass letting my muscle test gather dust. She gets off work at three thirty, for cripe's sake! She could have given me my A the same day I took the test.

With all the waiting I've had to do lately, I spend as much time outside as I can. For one thing, I eat lunch outside a lot at school. The weather's been nice, and even just being out there in the sun and wind clears my brain. Any worries I have get vacuumed right out.

Today Eric, Patrick, Stu, and I are sitting near the top of the bleachers. The guys are eating sandwiches from Carshon's. I've already finished mine. I'm stretched out across three rows, my equipment bag on the footboard under me while I wait for the guys to be done so we can hit a few balls, or toss a few back and forth, or whatever.

I love days like this—out-the-classroom-window kind of days. The sun is out, but it's fall so it's not too hot, and the breeze feels like it's going to lift you off the bleachers, just pick you up and float you away.

The other guys are eating really slow, and Eric's going on about his grandma, or maybe it's his sister, I'm not really sure. It's always whoever's fucking up his family the most at the moment. Whatever. If I'm not worried about *my* worries, I'm sure not worried about Eric's.

"Either my parents've got to give up their room," Eric's saying, "or they're going to have to build a bathroom next to the family room and put in doors and everything."

I only halfway listen. I'm noticing that the old backstop way back by the farthest fence is completely gone now. It was mostly gone before—there were just a couple of steel posts sticking out of the ground. But now there's not even that. Now nobody would even know that used to be a field.

Too bad; that's where my coach called practices when I was a little kid, on my first team. That's where I learned that there are places where nobody cares if you can sound out words or not.

"I don't see why they can't put her in Christine's room." Eric takes another bite of his sandwich. "I mean, Grandma could make it up the stairs if she really tried," he adds with his mouth full. "And we could take her meals up to her. That way she'd be guaranteed a visitor at least three times a day. And why would she ever have to come back down? It's not like she's got a life."

Patrick and I nod agreement, although I haven't really been listening and I'm sure Patrick hasn't either. Stu opens his mouth to say something, but then he shuts it real quick, because here comes Max Gutterson, the senior, walking around the corner of the refreshment stand. Max is carrying an equipment bag. Only the bag's moving, and it's making these ungodly yowling sounds.

There's a cat in there.

We all stare at the bag. Eric's been talking nonstop since we sat down out here—but looking at that bag, he doesn't have much to say all of a sudden.

"That the cat that's been hanging around all the time?" I ask Gutterson. Because I heard some of the cheerleader girls saying how they've been feeding this cute kitty that lives under the concession stand. I've also heard some of the guys complain how some stray cat's been shitting in the dirt around home plate.

"Right now it is," says Gutterson.

The bag twists and quivers and yowls. You got to wonder how it can breathe in there.

"We've all cleaned crap out of our cleats for the last time," Gutterson adds. "Gimme a bat, Trammel." He doesn't say please. He just reaches toward the bag at my feet.

"Fuck, no." I put my foot on the bag. Eric, Patrick, and Stu say nothing. Patrick, I know, likes cats. But he's stuck between liking cats and having one very big, very mean senior on his ass for the rest of the year.

Me, I don't care about cats one way or the other.

There's just no way Gutterson can order me around like that.

"Come on, Trammel," says Gutterson. "Don't be a—"

"Put it in the freezer," I say. "In the concession stand. Let 'em find it in the spring."

I don't know why I said it. I didn't even really think it—it just popped into my head. I'm actually a little shocked, that it came out of my mouth like that. Fortunately, I'm still sitting there with just the right amount of coolness, like Hey, whatever.

Gutterson grins. He never thought of that. The concession stand's locked up. But rumor has it there's a key. Rumor has it that more than one girl's buffed the concession stand floor with her back, courtesy of certain members of the varsity team.

Gutterson's staring at me. "You are one sick little bastard," he tells me with approval.

I shrug. I don't figure Gutterson'll really do it. I don't figure he's one of the guys with a key. Now Palmer, I'm sure, has one. But Gutterson would have been bragging about it all the time if he had one.

Gutterson disappears to the back of the concession stand. I can hear the sound of a key in the padlock, and then a *bang!* as the door swings all the way open against the wall.

Eric and Patrick and Stu are just sitting there, suddenly

silent. Eric and Stu are very interested in their shoes, but Patrick's staring at the concession stand, and he looks really miserable. Of course, he's not going to do anything about it. None of them are. That's my crew for you. They're afraid to help the cat, but still they've got to make me stop and think about what I just started.

All of them, Patrick especially, are sitting there ruining my peace of mind, rubbing it in that I was the one who said to put the cat in there. And the thing is, they'll probably all be moping around for days when all one of us has got to do is take a beating for the cat. Or maybe get put into the freezer himself for a little while. If he'd fit. I don't know how big it is, I just know they got room for hot dogs back there.

Finally we hear the sound of the door closing, and the scrabble and click of the lock, and Gutterson appears again.

"Great idea, Trammel," Gutterson says. "You may turn out not to be a total waste of space after all."

Then he's walking back up toward the school with an empty equipment bag.

One frozen kitty, coming up.

"How long do you think it'll live?" Patrick mutters to me.

"What am I, a vet?" I'm leaning back with my elbows on the bench behind me. It's a nice day for October. Not too breezy. Warm in the sun.

Out here, that is.

Okay, now I'm actually thinking about the stupid cat. About what it'd be like to freeze to death. Little paws on the cold, cold ice. Little meows in the dark. With nobody to hear.

"Hey," I tell the guys. "Freezing to death beats getting your skull bashed in with a baseball bat."

Nobody says anything.

"Freezing's just like falling asleep," I insist. I really think I heard that somewhere. Although I don't know how anybody would know—if you froze to death, you wouldn't be able to tell anybody how it felt because you'd be dead.

"It's too late now," Eric says, almost to himself. "There's no way to get in there anyway. Not without a key."

Not without a key.

"There might be," I point out.

"What do you mean?"

"We could beat the lock off with one of my bats."

None of them look relieved. They were trying to talk themselves into not feeling guilty, and now I ruined it for them.

"Gutterson thinks he's such hot shit," I say, because now my thoughts are bounding off in a completely different direction. "He needs to be taught a lesson."

Stu twists around and peers back up toward the building. The back of the concession stand's within clear view of two classrooms. "It'll be too loud," he says, but I'm already slipping off the bleachers onto the ground. I was starting to feel bad about mouthing off, but now I can ruin Gutterson's stupid plan. Ha ha.

But I'll have to hurry, because I don't know how much time we have till the bell rings and people start flooding out of the building for second lunch.

I unzip my bag and look over my bats. I select my oldest, cheapest bat, an Easton aluminum, to do the job. Nobody else moves. "Let me know if anybody's coming," I say, and walk around to the back of the concession stand to get to work.

Beating a padlock is not the same as hitting baseballs. A couple of minutes later my hands are hurting and my shoulders are sore from absorbing the shock. If the cat's still alive, it's probably shit all over the hot dogs from the racket.

I stop and check the padlock. Not even dented. I lower my bat.

"No go," I call to the guys, although I can't see them. "Sayonara, Kitty," I say lightly, like it doesn't matter, but then all of a sudden I'm swinging the bat around for one last really vicious whack to the lock.

And with that last whack, the screws that hold the hinge onto the door pop halfway out.

I act like I meant for that to happen. I put the bat down, pry the screws out with my fingers, and pull the door open.

It's dark in the concession stand. I make my way into the back, where they keep the boxes of food. I give my eyes a minute to adjust, and when they do, I see there's a huge triple sink and a refrigerator. A freezer.

I reach for the handle and pull the freezer door open.

Rrrow! A cold taffy-colored blur bursts into my face, slices across my right upper lip, and shoots out the door.

I've just released Freddy Krueger's cat. And now I'm standing alone in this dark room in front of an empty freezer. I touch my lip, gently. I can't tell if it's bleeding. It feels like the mother of all paper cuts on my face.

I edge back over to the door that leads outside. I lean around to peek out.

The grass is empty. The asphalt is empty. The classroom windows are blank.

The bleachers are empty too.

My friends are yellow-bellied dipshits.

I step out, shut the door to the concession stand. How many minutes till the bell?

I poke each screw back in its hole. The wood's splintered, and the screws keep falling back out. I finally have to give up. I pick up my bat, stick it back in my bag. I sling the whole thing over my shoulder and walk, very casually, up the slope toward the parking lot. The back of my shirt is wet from the sweat I worked up hammering on the lock. My lip stings from the cat scratch.

The bell rings right as I'm slipping onto the breezeway. Then I'm walking down the hall to my locker, so I can get my English book. I duck my head when Max Gutterson passes, so he doesn't see the mark I know is there, on my face.

I don't mind much that my friends were afraid. They're my friends, after all, and this kind of thing is why I have the rep I do. Besides, I like danger, and I got to destroy school property and save a helpless animal all at the same time!

I'm a fucking hero.

Not for long. On the way up the stairs to assistant, it occurs to me: What if somebody sees the broken lock? What if somebody saw me from the windows and puts two and two together? What if it gets back to Vice Principal Sheridan that I had something to do with busting the door open?

If Mom had a cow over bad grades, she'll come un-fucking-glued if I get suspended.

I can't work on my English now. I can't even open the

book. I plunk myself down in a chair a few seats down from Chlorophyll, who's reading, as usual. I scowl at the table, because I'm pretty pissed at myself. I don't know how I get mixed up in stuff like this.

Chlorophyll doesn't look up or say hello. She never says anything to me—except when I go first, and even then I have to poke her, or say "Hey." We've been in here alone every day for three weeks now, so I know her, I know that's how she is. Doesn't give a shit about anybody but herself.

Her book isn't a textbook today. It's a regular book. But she's actually *marking* on the pages. With a pencil, writing notes in the margins. Writing in a book that's already filled up with words. Figures.

I turn sideways, so I can look out the window. I can't see the concession stand from here, but now I'm realizing my fingerprints are probably all over it. Sheridan could call it more than breaking a hinge. He could call it breaking and entering.

I could get arrested.

How can everything get to be such a mess in a few short minutes of brainlock?

"I'm such a dumb fuck." I mutter it out loud. I can't help it. It's so true, it has to be *announced*.

"No impulse control."

It's Chlo. I look over. Her eyes just keep moving down

the page. I thought she was off in her book world. When she's like that, she could be a chair or a part of the table. She could probably sit here all day and never notice if the roof blew off.

And she must have been talking to her book, because for somebody who just butted in, she doesn't seem at all interested.

Impulse control. What does that mean? *Was* she talking to me? She's not explaining—it's like she doesn't even know she said it.

I think about it, looking out the window again. Then I turn around in my chair and stare at the tabletop for a few minutes. I'm trying to figure it out. "You mean I don't control my impulses," I say, and as soon as it's out of my mouth, I know it sounds dumb. But it makes sense, somehow, to say it that way.

"Maybe." Now she gives me one of those librarian looks, over her glasses. "But then, I don't know you. Could be you are just a dumb fuck."

I aim one quick glare at her—what's she doing listening to me all of a sudden?—but she's got her eyes down again, and I'm too depressed to start anything with anybody right now.

Somebody left a pencil stub on the table. I pick it up and start digging my name into the tabletop.

"Maybe," I hear Chlorophyll say, and when I glance

over, I see that she's staring at the page without really seeing it, "maybe they mean the same thing. What is a dumb fuck but someone who doesn't think before he acts?"

I get her point. It's me. No matter what you call it. "It sounds better to call it no impulse control," I say, grinding the pencil into the curve of the *o* in Colt.

Chlorophyll doesn't say anything. She's just staring and thinking. She's forgotten that this is about *me*.

It's too bad. For a minute there she could have almost passed for a human being.

I realize I just carved my name in the table, where Miss A. will see it. And tell Coach. "Listen," I say as I turn the pencil over and try to erase the letters. "Don't tell anybody I called myself a dumb fuck. You hear?"

Chlo's pencil is hovering over her book. She's completely spaced.

I stop erasing and lean over the table. *"Hey!"* She blinks. "You hear? Don't tell anybody what I said."

She gives me that look. The over-the-glasses one.

"What's your name again? Terrell?"

God, what planet is she from? "It's *Trammel*," I tell her.

"Trammel. That's right. Trammel, don't flatter yourself. I don't care what you do or don't do. I don't care what any of your smarmy little high school friends do or don't do. No one in this rathole is even a blip on my radar screen. Especially you, Trammel. You mean nothing to me. Nada. Zip."

She goes back to her reading and marking.

And I go back to my erasing. What she said actually makes me feel better. I guess if you had a college boyfriend, you really *wouldn't* care about high-school stuff. So I don't have to worry about her repeating anything.

Erasing does nothing. I dug in too hard.

"Just make sure you keep your mouth shut," I warn her anyway, and I try one more scrub of the eraser before giving up. My name's just there, that's all. For all eternity. Maybe they'll think some other Colt wrote it.

"Don't worry your pretty little head, Terrell," she mutters.

"Trammel."

"Whatever."

Okay, so nobody's going to know that I was calling myself names like a psycho. That's good.

I toss the pencil stub in the trash. Now all I have to worry about is Gutterson finding out what I did with the cat—because if he does, he's going to kick my ass so hard, I'll be biting my own butt every time I shut my mouth.

• • •

Sixth period. Okay. I can bullshit my way through this.

And if that doesn't work, I have to at least show no fear when Gutterson kills me.

I take a deep breath and walk into athletics acting real casual. Go sit at the machine for some traps work. Like, hey, it's just another day.

Palmer and Gutterson heading to the leg press first, as usual. They're talking, as usual. The only thing that's not usual is that before they get started breaking each other's kneecaps, Gutterson speaks to me.

"Hey Trammel," he says, and I freeze inside, but my outside, thank God, just reaches forward and sets the key between the plates. "You see anybody heading toward the concession stand after I left?"

Oh. My. God.

Inside, I'm about to pee my boxers.

Outside, where it counts, I'm totally cool. "No," I say, exactly right, not too quick, not too slow. "Why?"

"Somebody let the fucking cat out," Gutterson complains.

"No way. You just put it in there!"

"I know. That's why I was wondering if you saw anybody."

"No." I reach up, grab the handles on the bar, but I don't pull them down yet. I'm thinking. "How do you know it's gone?" I ask, and start my first set.

Gutterson talks while I pull the bar down to my shoulder blades, lots of control so the plates don't bang, knees straining against the pads, pulleys squeaking. "I told Simmons and Karinsky," he says, "and they thought I was bullshitting and went to check. They said there was nothing there. Somebody had to've let it out."

"It's your own fault," Palmer tells Gutterson. "You're the one who went and told everybody it was in there."

"I only told about five or six people besides Simmons and Karinsky. What good is it to do something cool if nobody knows you did it?"

Six. Seven. Eight.

I stand up to let the bar go, then sit back down. "That sucks. Whoever let it out," I tell Gutterson firmly, "should have his ass kicked."

"Maybe Simmons and Karinsky did it," Palmer says. "Just to make you look stupid. Or maybe the cat got out on its own. I know I'd be kicking the freezer door down, if it was me in there."

Gutterson shrugs. "At least they didn't snitch on me. Fuck it." He doesn't sound angry—he sounds disappointed that his work of art doesn't get to stand. "It was a good idea, though."

"Trammel's a good-idea man," Palmer says, approving. "Remember he went out the window a couple weeks ago? Hey," he adds, glancing at me. "What happened to your lip?"

"Paper cut," I tell him, easy.

"On your *face*?"

"Shut up, Palmer. I was licking an envelope," I add.

They both start laughing, just like I expected. Gutterson mimes me cutting my face open. I ignore them and reach to grab the bar again for my next set. This is working out better than I ever could have hoped. And it sure took my mind off my troubles for the day.

I just invented a new saying: Unfreezing cats makes the waiting go faster.

CHAPTER SIX

Keeping It All Under Control

Finally. In biology, Ms. Keller opens her briefcase and takes out a stack of papers.

"Hey," I call. "Are those the muscle tests?"

"Yes," says Ms. Keller.

"Thank God," I say, as she starts handing them back. "You've had them since the dinosaurs lived." Now I've got something that'll cheer me up for the whole rest of the day. An A! Wow. I hope Mom doesn't have a heart attack.

I sit up straight in my seat, watching Ms. Keller distribute each paper. The stack gets smaller and smaller in her hands. For the first time ever, I think it's too bad teachers don't call the grades out loud, for everybody to hear.

And then she's in front of Chlo and me, and I can see the red number even as it's coming toward me over the tabletop.

60

I take the test in my hand. Right underneath the 60 it says:

These are not the complete Latin terms.

I wad the test into a ball. I stand up right in front of Ms. Keller and do a rim shot off Alicia Doghead, who is sharpening her pencil. The balled-up test hits Alicia in the butt, and bounces off into the trash can. All this right under Ms. Keller's nose.

A couple of people snicker; Alicia turns to see what hit her. She sees me glaring and scurries back to her desk. Ms. Keller says, "Colt," in a warning tone, but I don't care. I don't look Ms. Keller's way again the whole period.

I should have known better than to think I could get a break. I should have known better than to get excited about a stupid fucking test. Even though out of all the people in this room, I'm probably the only one who really *does* know this stuff, because I'm the only one who actually *uses* it.

But I don't know the goddamn *Latin*.

It's so fucking unfair.

• • •

In fourth-period English Hammond hands back our pop quizzes. The one on Coltridge and Woolsworth.

Hammond always folds papers in half before he hands them back, so nobody can see your grade. Across the top of mine, in red ink, it says:

Are these your own ideas? You start sentences but don't finish them. In the ones you do finish, your points aren't clear. Also, you contradict yourself in several places—see starred remarks.

And right below that, still in red ink but even bigger, big as a billboard for anybody to see:

50

Does this day suck or what?

I bring my English book to fifth-period assistant. I've been thinking, and I'm pretty sure I've got the way to use Chlorophyll to help me pass. All I need is a 70 average, after all.

She comes in and sits down. "Hey," I ask her real casual, before she can pull out her book. "My mom said I should get a tutor, and I was thinking. You remember much about last year's English?"

"Some."

"You be interested in helping me study for a test coming up? I'd pay you—it wouldn't have to be free or anything."

"I thought you were the cheating type."

She thought right. I'm hoping I can get her to write down the important stuff for me. Then later I can copy it onto a little piece of paper and tuck it into my watch-band or something. She'll never have to know.

And as far as my mom is concerned, I'll be passing all on my own.

"It's going to be an essay test," I tell her. "It's hard to cheat on those." It *is*; I'll have to take those little tiny cheat sheets and turn them into a whole essay. "Hard to cheat *well*, anyway," I admit.

"Nice to know you take pride in your work." She unzips her backpack. Pulls out a book.

"So," I say, before she can open it. "What do you think?"

She pauses, hand on the cover. "How much?"

"I don't know. What seems fair?"

She stares down at her book. The title is two long words I can't read upside down—and probably not right side up either. "I don't know. I don't really need any money."

I start to make some crack about paying her with sex, but I actually control the impulse. I'm learning.

"How about if we come up with terms later?" she says.

I'm not sure what terms are, but I figure she means payment. And what that means is when later comes, I won't pay at all. Sounds like a good deal to me.

"Okay," I agree.

"What are you studying?"

I open the book, pull out the paper I stuck in to mark the place. I slide it around so she can see it. "This."

"Romantic poets."

"Yeah."

She puts her hand over the page so I can't see. "Do you remember any of their names?"

"No," I tell her.

She moves her hand. "Wordsworth, Coleridge, Keats, Byron, Shelley."

I shrug.

"What'd the teacher tell you about them?"

I shrug again.

"They didn't tell you the interesting stuff, then. If they had, you'd've remembered."

"I doubt it."

She's getting this *smile*. Almost . . . sinister. I don't know if I like it or not. "Byron got kicked out of England for screwing everything in sight. Other men's wives, boys, his own sister."

"Oh, God," I say in disgust.

"Does that bother you?"

"*Yes,*" I say. "God, his *sister*—I don't even want to think about it."

"What, the boy part's okay with you?"

"*God*, no," I say. "Will you shut up?"

"Sure," she says. "Because now you'll remember who Byron was. He was the letch." She taps her finger on the book. "The interesting thing is his poems are pretty pure. Like this one. 'She Walks in Beauty.'"

She starts to read, and her voice deepens and slows.

> *"She walks in beauty, like the night*
> *Of cloudless climes and starry skies;*
> *And all that's best of dark and bright*
> *Meet in her aspect and her eyes."*

She stops and looks at me, across the table. I feel embarrassed all of a sudden, like I just saw her shaving her legs.

So I get down to business. "Okay." I tear off a thick strip from the bottom of one of the leftover school newspapers and grab one of Miss A.'s pens. "So what do I have to know about it for the test?"

"How should I know? Probably you'd better just understand it. It's about his cousin, his girl cousin, with dark hair and dark eyes. He saw her this one time, at a party, and she was wearing a black dress with diamond sparkles all over it. And she was so beautiful, it stuck in his mind and he wrote this about her."

"Did he screw her, too?"

"I don't think so." Chlorophyll looks at me over the rim of her glasses. "But that's not the point. The point is haven't you ever seen somebody who was so beautiful that the moment stuck in your mind like a picture?"

"No," I say, although Grace pops into my head. "Have you?"

"Of course."

"When?"

"Do you want to learn about Byron, or not?"

"Yeah," I say. "Actually, no. My head is kind of full right now. Do you mind if we take a break?"

"Sure." She doesn't give my book back. She starts reading the rest of the Byron page.

I watch her for a few minutes. She's very strange-looking, she's a nobody, and she can be somewhat of a bitch—but I can't help thinking Grace would've had a cow if I'd asked if Byron had nailed his cousin.

"Hey," I say. "Chlo." I remember now her name's Corinne, but I don't want her to get the idea we're buddies or anything. "Really. Whose picture sticks in your mind?"

She doesn't look up, but her eyes stop moving down the page. "Brian."

"Byron?"

"Brian. My boyfriend."

"He have dark hair and eyes?"

"Yeah."

"He wear a dress with diamonds?"

She looks up at me, and she actually gives a little laugh. "No, he doesn't."

"My girlfriend, she's blond."

Chlo nods, but then she goes back to reading Byron. Lost interest again. So I feel free to think my own thoughts.

"She doesn't have dark eyes." I'm thinking out loud. "But she wore a black dress to the Valentine's Day dance last year. It wasn't a date—she wasn't allowed to date back then—but there was a bunch of us went together and I got to dance with her most of the time. Her dress had these sparkly things on it. They sort of looked like diamonds."

Chlo doesn't even nod this time.

"She looked great," I say, "so I can kind of see the thing about the black, and the diamonds. It's too bad there's nothing in that poem about smell," I go on, "because she was wearing some kind of perfume—usually she doesn't wear any—but the day after the dance I was hanging up my jacket, and I could still smell her perfume on it."

Just thinking about it, I feel like I could almost smell Grace, if I tried—and then I realize I'm breathing deep, through my nose like an idiot. I look at Chlo real quick.

She's just looking at me, straight-faced, like she didn't notice.

Still, I feel my face getting hot.

"You two been going out long?" she asks me.

I want to spit out something rude—because I know my face is red and I don't like the way she saw me sniffing the air like a horny bloodhound.

But I can't be rude. Because she knows her stuff and I need what she knows, to pass English.

"Awhile." I look down at the paper. It's empty—there's nothing on it whatever about Lord Byron. I crumple it up and lean back in my chair, shooting for the wastebasket in the corner.

A perfect shot. I raise my arms in victory, and bang my chair back down.

Back to business.

"So," I say, "what do you say to being my tutor? I'll pay you," I remind her, because in spite of what she said about not needing money, she really looks like she could use it. "All you have to do is tell me what I need to know for the test."

She shakes her head.

"We're halfway there," I tell her. "Already I remember

Byron's the one who screws anything that moves and he wrote the poem about his beautiful cousin in the black dress with the diamonds on it."

She shakes her head again. "I don't think so."

"Come on. There's nothing else to do in here. I won't tell anybody you're tutoring me, and you won't tell anybody either. Your boyfriend doesn't even have to know," I add, in case that's what's worrying her. "And you'll be making *mon-ey*," I sing, to really pile it on.

"Okay," Chlo says. "All right. But I can't promise anything. All I can do is give you the info. The rest is up to you."

"You're on," I tell her.

It isn't until the bell rings, and I'm already out the door, that I realize she might think she's got a right to come up and talk to me in the hall now.

But then I have to laugh.

I practically have to set myself on fire in front of her to get her to even glance at me.

And strangely enough, that makes me feel better.

Later, after dinner, I'm actually studying. Mom's at the computer, Cass and her friend Anne-Marie are in her room working on some project. Me and Cass are in the usual truce we have when either of us has friends over. I guess neither of us wants anybody to know how stupid we act when it's just us.

Me, I'm standing at the kitchen counter holding my English book open with one palm flat on the page, while I stuff salsa-flavored crackers in my mouth with the other hand. I'm looking at a picture of Byron. He's got some weird thing on his head, can't figure out what it is. Looks like a wadded-up curtain. There's "She Walks in Beauty." "Canto from Don Juan."

The actual words don't make much sense, of course. I check my watch, eat a few more crackers. Look at the words some more. Now I'm thinking about Grace.

I wish Grace could see me right now. Reading poetry and all. She'd be impressed as hell.

So I call her. "I don't really need anything," I say. "I was just reading a little Byron, and thought I'd call."

Silence. I can't tell if it's an impressed silence.

"So," I ask Grace, "Whatcha doing?"

Turns out Grace is about to sit down and watch a DVD she borrowed from Ashley, her friend who's in drama *and* she's a cheerleader. Ashley is a crossover.

I'd like to ask if I can come over and watch the movie with Grace, but no way do I want to watch it at her house, with her dad breathing down my neck to make sure I don't get any fingerprints on his daughter.

"Hey," I tell her, "why don't you bring it over here? I'd like to see . . . what is it?"

"*Beauty and the Beast.* Remember you were talking about it? You made me want to see it again."

"Oh." The cartoon? Holy shit. "Great. I love that movie."

"You're kidding."

"No," I lie. "It's one of my favorites."

Silence. "Gosh. You're full of surprises." She sounds like that's a good thing. "But," she adds, "you know my dad won't—"

"My mom is home."

"Oh." Grace's dad knows and trusts my mom. He knows my mom has a thing about good lighting and frequent family-room checks.

I don't put my English book away because I want Grace to see it.

The movie Grace brings is *not* the cartoon. It's an old black-and-white thing.

With subtitles.

Oh God.

It's pretty weird, although not the weirdest thing she ever made me see. The trophy has to go to this thing called *Eraserhead,* about a guy with hair like a pencil eraser and this chick with cheeks the size of grapefruit who comes out of the radiator and sings about heaven. I mean, I couldn't even fall asleep during it, it was so weird.

This one, though, it's got a story. I just don't know what it is because it's in a foreign language. I'm pretty sure it's along the same lines as the cartoon, though, because it's got a beautiful lady in a big-skirted dress and a guy with beast-type makeup on. And I know it's a romance, because Grace's got that same soft-eyed, almost-crying look she gets during epic smooch fests, where for the next few days it's like you're being measured against some pretty-boy actor who got his lines written for him, while you're on your own.

I put my arm along the back of the couch, not actually around Grace, but as close as I can get without Mom coming in and clearing her throat at me. And after a while Grace is up against me, leaning against my chest. Looks like saying I love this movie gained me some points. All lights are on, of course. Still, to be with Grace I'd sit bolt upright watching a movie in Swahili, if it came down to it.

The only problem comes when Cass and Anne-Marie pass through on their way to get food, and stop to watch.

"What are they saying?" Anne-Marie asks us.

I don't answer because I don't know.

"Read the subtitles," Grace says without looking around. Grace loves animals, and she waves to losers in the hall, but she doesn't have much patience with people who ask stupid questions.

Right then the Beast speaks. The whole screen's just this dude in cheap makeup and plastic fangs, saying over and over in this growly voice, "La Behhhll. La Behhhhll. La Behhhhll."

Anne-Marie and Cass start giggling.

"La Behhhll," growls the Beast.

The awful thing is, it *is* funny. When it's just me and Grace, it's easy to forget that I'm watching this goofy guy in pantaloons and fake fur who sounds like Pepe LePew. But with Cass and Anne Marie here, I can't help but remember how stupid it is.

I bite the inside of my cheek so I don't start smiling.

"La Behhll," Beast says.

"La Behhll," Cass growls behind us. Giggle giggle.

I could kill them both. But if I say anything, it'll come out as a laugh. I stare hard at the TV.

"La Behhll," the girls growl in unison. My chest begins to shake with laughter.

Grace can feel it. She sits up and turns to look at me.

"I'm sorry," I tell her as my face cracks into a smile. "God, I'm sorry. It's just . . ."

"La Behhlll," Beast growls again.

Grace reaches over me and picks up the remote from the arm of the couch. She hits the pause button. "You all just let me know when you're finished."

Her eyes hit me like a laser beam.

I think it's the way I *don't* look at Cass that tells her she better get the hell out of here. "Come on," she tells Anne-Marie, "bring the Oreos."

Then they're gone, and the Beast's face is taking up the whole screen, his mouth open right in the middle of "La Behhll." I look over at Grace, but she's not looking at me now.

She's mad again.

"Sorry 'bout laughing." I don't want her to be mad. If she's going to be mad, it should be for stuff she doesn't even know about, like feeling up Silver and getting hot for Whorey Dori. Not for the stuff she *does* know about, like Coke-can rings and laughing at a movie.

But Grace won't even look at me. She's just staring at the TV, even though it's paused. And all she says is, "Are you ready to *watch* now?"

This movie would be a lot more realistic if, instead of standing around growling into the camera, the Beast got his leg caught in a trap and had to gnaw his own paw off. Because that's how I feel sometimes with Grace.

"Yeah," I tell Grace, who isn't leaning against me anymore. "Start 'er up."

WEEK FOUR

CHAPTER SEVEN

Just a Little Bit Crooked

Tuesday morning in biology, Alicia Doghead's backpack is in the aisle, so I step squarely on it and over, like it's a stepping stone. I hear Alicia mutter something, and when I look around, she's glaring at me—but I give her a cold stare, and she looks away.

Chlo's sitting there at the table, as usual. She's not wearing jeans or pants for once. Instead she's got on this denim skirt. But it's not straight along the bottom hem, like every other skirt in the world. It's like she's wearing a big square of cloth, it's got *corners*, somehow—it's got *points* along the bottom, and each point ends in a clip-hook, like you'd use to clip a flashlight to your belt loop.

I'm looking her over, and I see she's got on her usual baggy top, a sweater of some kind. But that skirt! Halfway down her skirt there's these metal *rings* sewn on—one about a foot above every corner, each hook. So she can clip her skirt up, I guess.

It occurs to me that if she'd dress decent, I might even like her okay. But I can't afford to like her, because she's just too fucking weird.

It pisses me off.

I want to start something with her, but I don't dare, because of the English thing, and because she knows too much about me. So I kind of halfway start messing with her, but not really.

"So Chlo," I say, "you think you and me ought to go out sometime?"

"No."

"We could. You could wear that. I like that—what is it? A tent?"

"It's a skirt."

"Where'd you get it? Army Navy?"

"Thrift store."

I forgot, she's poor. But that doesn't mean you have to dress like a pool cover.

"No kidding," I tell her. "Hey, I could go down to the thrift store, get something to match. We could go camping."

"No."

"We can't go out at all?"

"No."

"Because of your *boyfriend*?"

"That, and because we wouldn't have anything to talk about."

"We could talk about *poetry*."

"You mean I'd talk, and you'd write it down."

"We could talk about baseball."

"I don't know anything about baseball."

"I could talk," I tell her, "and *you* could write it down."

She's stacking her papers, all business. Then she sets them down and gives me a look. "Why would I want to write it down?"

"Because it's interesting."

"No it's not."

"Yeah it is. It's like poetry. Only you live it."

She looks at me. "How's it like poetry?"

"It just *is*, that's all."

"Describe it."

"I don't describe it," I tell her. "I just do it."

"One word, then. If you could describe it in one word, what would it be?"

"Power," I say without thinking. "No. Control. Hell, I don't know. Bat, ball, glove. You're the fucking writer, not me."

Somehow, this is turning out not to be fun. Somehow I lost charge of the conversation.

"Quit talking to me, Chlo," I tell her. She's always mixing me up.

• • •

In English, Mr. Hammond gives me a three-week
failure notice that I'm supposed to take home. My grade
is 53. I'm going to have to save my mom from a stroke
by forging her signature.

I'm not too worried. Not yet. That 53 is just a warning
before the real grade. It's a scare tactic. I don't scare
easy, but my mom might not understand that I can bring
it up before the final report.

She wouldn't understand that three weeks is plenty of
time.

In fifth period Chlo comes in all hot to tutor. She
plunks her backpack on the table and sits down. "I was
thinking back," she says, pulling my English book
toward her. "There's one of these poems that you might
like."

That gets my attention. "*Like?* As in . . . not mind reading it?"

"Yeah." She looks at me over her glasses. "That a
problem?"

I grin. "Nope. Tell you what—I'll pay you extra if I *like*
it. How's that? Double. Triple. Hell, I'll buy you a car if
I like this poem you picked out."

She reads it out loud. I zone out about a third of the
way in.

"The Tables Turned

"Up! up! my Friend, and quit your books;
Or surely you'll grow double:
Up! up! my Friend, and clear your looks:
Why all this toil and trouble?

"The sun, above the mountain's head,
A freshening lustre mellow
Through all the long green fields has spread,
His first sweet evening yellow.

"Books! 'tis a dull and endless strife:
Come, hear the woodland linnet,
How sweet his music! on my life,
There's more of wisdom in it.

"And hark how blithe the throstle sings!
Blah-de-blah-de-blah . . ."

At some point Chlo's voice stops droning on, and then after a couple more seconds she asks, "Well?"

I give my slow, wise nod. "In my opinion," I say, very intellectually, "this poem sucks so bad that they should burn every copy of it ever made. I hate it. It's the most stupid thing I ever—"

"Okay, I hear you. Point taken. But don't you get what it's about?"

"Duh! No! That's why you're here. Hello, anybody home?"

"It says that you don't need to learn from books, when you can go outside and learn about life that way. 'Books! 'tis a dull and endless strife'—get it?"

"Yeah, I get it. Dull and endless—I sure get *that*."

"I can't believe you don't like the idea it's expressing."

"Look. It took you about, I don't know, what, six words? to say what takes him a whole page, and you don't use words like . . ." I bend over the page " . . . thros-tull. What the fuck is a throstle?"

"It's a bird."

"Why write about some bird that nobody ever heard of and everybody's got to look up?"

"Everybody doesn't have to look it up, some people know it, plus you can get it from the context—"

"Everybody who's normal's got to look it up. What's the name of the guy who wrote this?"

"William Wordsworth."

"He's a dipshit."

Chlo shakes her head. "You know what the problem is? You've already decided you're not going to like it."

"I have not."

"Yeah, you have. You're sitting there like, 'Make this

entertaining over my dead body.'"

"I don't care if it's entertaining or not. I just want to *pass*."

"I know. It's such a wasted opportunity, though. Especially this poem. It's *so* you! Remember when you climbed out the window in biology?"

I lean back, smiling. "Yeah."

"And the rest of us were stuck inside."

"Hey, seize the day, right?"

"At first I thought you were crazy, but then I saw you out there playing baseball, and I was sitting there doing mindless rote work, and I thought, Now there's a man who knows what's important."

"I sure do."

"Not quite. Otherwise you'd put more effort into studying."

"I put a *lot* of effort into studying. I spent all last night looking at Byron. I *do* study," I say again. "It's just that teachers don't like me. Plus . . ." My voice dies off. I actually almost said that I'm not too good at this stuff.

"Plus what?"

"Plus . . . it's just hard sometimes, that's all." Now she's going to tell me it's not hard, that I need to apply myself. That's what they always say.

But she doesn't say it.

She just shrugs. "Different people are good at different

things. Maybe English isn't your cup of tea. Unfortunately, we all have to get through it if we want to keep our options open."

"You mean like a career."

"I mean like being thirty-five and spending your days mopping rest rooms at Taco Bell."

"Nah. I'd be the one working the register."

"I wouldn't trust you with a drawer full of money."

"I wouldn't either, but the guys at Taco Bell don't know that."

"Anyway, Trammel, you should try to keep in mind that whenever you get tired of studying and want to give up, this could be a lot worse. You could be wiping dried piss off the base of a public toilet. Makes Wordsworth sound a little better, huh?"

"Yeah, when you put it that way. But," I added, "I don't like the poem, and I'm not paying you a dime. For the bet, I mean," I add quickly. "I'll just pay the regular tutor amount. No offense," I add.

"None taken," she says.

I hate taking Cass to her dance class. First of all, it's boring, and second of all, it's a waste of my time.

But when Mom tells me she's got to work late all week, and I have to take Cass to dance lessons, I don't dare argue, because I don't want to piss Mom off until after baseball starts. So like a good brother I take my little sister in the pouring rain to her stupid dance lesson.

When I pull up in front of the studio, Cass gets out of the car and gets my seats all wet leaving the door open while she wrestles with her umbrella, even though the front door of the dance studio is less than five feet away. Then she walks off without even saying thank you. Little Miss Snot, if you ask me.

Now I've got fifty minutes to kill.

In the shopping center there's also a grocery store, a drugstore, a post office, a sandwich shop, a tailor, an insurance agent. The rest of the spaces are empty. I could go grab a sandwich, or I could go to the drugstore, look at magazines, or I could hang out and watch Cass and her friends dance.

Now some of Cass's friends are going to be real look-ers in a couple of years when they get some boobs. In fact, a few of them are well on the way. And I got to tell you those girls about fall all over themselves when I come into the room. Like I just walked off the cover of some teen magazine. Sometimes it makes me think how much easier life would be if I could fall for a younger girl. If I could ignore all the giggling and the junior-high stuff, like when insults mean you like somebody.

But no way would I ever be caught fishing around that

underdeveloped little pond called McMoore Middle School. How much more of a loser could I be?

So I decide I'm going to drive over to the drugstore, get a candy bar and a magazine. I drive slow, because it's one of those dark, windy storms, where it's really pouring down and the rain is sheeting up on the sidewalk.

I have to turn the defroster on because I can hardly see through the fogged-up window. The wipers are on full blast even as I'm edging along. I think I see somebody walking across the parking lot up ahead, but it's hard to tell.

When I finally take a swipe at the windshield with my sleeve, I see there is a person, and it's a girl. She's walking along with her back to me. No umbrella, just trudging away through the puddles, wet like a kitten somebody threw into a pond. She looks miserable. She looks cold. She looks . . .

Familiar.

Whorey Dori.

I've already slowed down without meaning to, I guess just because she looks so damn pitiful. I mean, out here all alone, and nobody ever talks to her even when she's dry.

Dori.

Now, letting her talk to me on the phone is one thing. Offering her a ride would be something else. Something

156

stupid! Jesus, she already thinks she's got the right to call me anytime she wants! She might figure I'm going to sponsor her back into the group.

The wipers go *tha-thump, tha-thump*.

So what if she's soaking wet? She's *so* soaking wet, it won't make a bit of difference if she gets out of the rain or not.

She ain't gonna drown, I tell myself.

But as I get closer, I see exactly *how* soaking wet she is. She's wearing a T-shirt, and her clothes are clinging to her body, her shirt's sticking to her.

Really sticking to her.

Every inch of her.

Now, here I am with fifty minutes to kill. And here's this soaking-wet girl who needs a ride and who—what a coincidence—is a known nympho.

I ease off the gas until I'm rolling along beside her. I crank down the window. The rain's beating on my head while I yell, "You need a ride somewhere?"

She doesn't recognize me right away. She squints at me for a second—then it comes over her face, I'm Colt, her phone pal—and she splashes around to the passenger side.

When she gets in, the smell of rain and wet cloth comes in with her, and her hair is clinging to her cheeks and neck, her clothes are clinging everywhere.

Now, of course I'm in love with Grace. Who by the way has never done one single thing to relieve any of my tension, if you know what I mean. She always acts like I've got a snake down my pants.

And it's not like I'm going to actually do anything wrong. Not officially. There's other things you can do besides the Deed Itself.

In other words, it's pretty junior high to sit at home alone and polish the old bayonet if you can find a living breathing girl willing to do it for you.

Look at it this way: Everybody puts gas in their car, right? And when they go to a gas station, they can either use self-service or let somebody else do it for them. It doesn't matter, the end result is the same: A full tank— and it's strictly personal preference how it got that way. End of story.

If I had to take a guess, I'd say hormones had something to do with this. It's been a while since I've had a fill-up.

"Thanks, Colt," Dori's saying, breathless. Her shirt is too dark to see through, but she must be cold because her nipples are sticking out like those 3D dots that blind people can read.

Which you're *supposed* to run your fingers over, by the way.

Dori looks at me and smiles, and I see that her eyeliner, or whatever that black stuff is, is smeared under her eyes. The moment she looks out the window at all that rain, I look at her breasts again, the way they vibrate as the car moves along, at her nipples poking at her shirt, like . . . like . . .

Like two blips of Morse code, saying: *Do! Me!*

And really, that's reasonable. Forget the kid stuff. I *ought* to just go ahead and do her. For Grace's sake, of course—it'll be better for both of us if I rack up some experience first. That way there won't be a lot of fumbling around. I mean, I know what to do—how difficult could it be? But practicing on Dori will help me build up some finesse. Like in baseball—you don't go straight to regular season. No, you need a couple of practice games first, to work out the bugs, improve your technique. Find your rhythm.

"I didn't know you lived around here," Dori is saying.

"I don't. My sister takes dance right over there."

"Oh." She nods.

I don't know what to say next. So I nod too, and then we're both nodding. I hadn't figured on having to make conversation.

I haven't seen Dori in person in a long time. I'd forgotten how she really is pretty fine. With a *very* fine rack. Although the way her eyes are smeared with that black stuff makes it look like she's been crying.

"Looks like you got caught in the rain," I tell her.

"Yeah. I had to take something to the post office. It couldn't wait."

I almost wonder what it is that's so important she's got to mail it in the rain. But I don't *want* to. I don't want to wonder anything at all about Dori. "So," I say, "which way am I going?"

"Straight ahead. It's only about a block." A drop of water runs down her cheek. She wipes it off with the back of her hand. "Turn here."

Now I'm driving down a street with little houses all lined up like shoe boxes.

"This is it," she says.

"This one?"

"Yeah."

I pull up in front of the shoe box she's pointing to. There's a saggy screen door, and the windows have aluminum foil to keep out the sun. I tell myself, What a lazy skanky family, to let your house look like that.

My hand reaches down slowly to kill the engine. But I'm looking at that house, and I'm getting this feeling, like there's a sign out front that says, *Hey, Colt—You Could Be Living Here*!

One night years ago, right after my dad moved out, I was coming down the stairs and heard my mom on the phone, yelling, "You just ask him where his children are supposed to live!" She was shrieking by the end of it, and it scared the hell out of me, watching her slam the phone down, and when she turned around there were tears coming down her cheeks.

She didn't know I was looking down at her the whole time, of course, and when she saw me huddled on the staircase, she stopped pacing and told me everything was okay, she was just a little late on the house payment but she'd never been late before and they'd give her a little leeway just this once. Then she sent me to bed, but I just lay there wide-awake, thinking we were about to get kicked out of our home that very night, and wondering if the police would come with flashing lights, and if I'd get to take any toys or clothes, and if they'd kick us out onto the sidewalk or take us to jail.

That should have been the end of it, but it wasn't. The next day my mom was on the phone again, probably with my dad but I don't know for sure, and when she slammed down the phone, her mouth was all pinched up and she said she was ready to haul ass to her own place, that she could afford all on her own. So she took me and Cass out with her while she looked at houses for sale—small, old houses, like this one.

I got to tell you I was scared shitless. On top of my parents hating each other, and my dad leaving, and my mother shrieking and crying, I was going to be forced to leave the only house in the only neighborhood I'd ever known.

The truth is, I know Dori's family probably doesn't have enough money to fix things, or to buy blinds.

But I say it again, to myself. Lazy. Skanky.

It doesn't help. I'm getting this urgent feeling, like if I don't get busy doing this girl right away, I'm going to start thinking too much, and blow this chance completely.

I don't know, could be I've got a funny expression, because Dori says suddenly, "Sorry about the way the house looks."

"Aw, no," I say quickly. "It's great."

"I live with my dad, and he's too busy to keep up with it on the outside. I've been working on the inside, though."

I nod, because I know she has been. "Wallpaper," I say.

"Yeah. Although I haven't actually saved up the money to buy any yet. I'm still kind of picking it out. So," Dori says, after another moment, "what all classes do you have right now?"

I pull my eyes away from that house, stare at the dashboard. I have to make myself think. "Biology. Tech ed. Geometry—"

"Tech ed? What period?"

"Second." My mother made me take it.

"I've got it third. Who do you have?"

"Wheeler."

"Oh. I've got Dixon. I'm going to try to get into work-study next year. You know, where you go to school in the morning and work in the afternoons? And I'm going to graduate early, if I can."

I nod.

She's watching me, for some kind of response, I guess. The windows are fogging up. I'm definitely starting to think too much. Better get things started.

Now.

Only I'm not really sure how to begin.

Kiss her, I think. But she's leaning back against the door—she's not situated right. So I look at her hand, flat on the seat beside her, and tell myself I'm going to take her hand and put it you-know-where. Then I tell myself how I'm just going to slide over there and put my hand on her breast. Although I know from experience that kind of thing usually doesn't go over too well. Most times you have to go through a bunch of other stuff first.

"I really appreciate how nice you've been to me, Colt."

Talk to her, I think. Tell her she's pretty. Tell her something! Speak, boy!

"Not just giving me a ride, but talking to me on the

phone and everything. You're really a good person. All those people like Stephanie and Preston and Ashley— they think they're so great just because of who they are and where they live and what they own. But you're the only one of them who's really decent inside."

Jesus. I don't know what to say to this girl. Not at all, and I don't know what to do with myself in front of this house.

"Listen, I'd ask you in," Dori's saying, "but my dad's asleep."

It's five o'clock in the afternoon. And I remember how Mom used to work weird hours for a while there, before she got into real estate.

"That's okay," I hear myself say.

"Anyway, thanks." Dori reaches for the door handle.

It's okay, I tell myself, Let her go. She's nobody. Anyway, your first shouldn't be Jordan Palmer's seconds. Grace Garcetti's going to be the one.

The door's open now—the rain has slacked off a little, it's just regular rain, not pelting—and Dori slides out.

But she doesn't leave. She bends over a little to look me in the eye.

"Colt, I know this sounds stupid, but if you ever need anything, I'm there for you. Girl trouble, anything. Even if you just need somebody to talk to. You've got my number."

But I don't think I do. I erased it every time she left it.

Finally she shuts the door. My palms are sweating. I watch her walk all the way to the porch, watch the screen door slam shut behind her. The screen door with a wrought-iron flamingo nailed into the frame.

I feel how I'm breathing too fast, I'm hyperventilating. Slow down, dude, I tell myself. Relax. You could have done her. You just didn't feel like it. You're in control. This is your show.

You're Colt Trammel, after all.

The first thing that's different I notice right away. As soon as I walk in the door of biology.

I don't say anything until after the bell rings and we're all supposed to be reading.

"You cut your hair," I whisper to Chlorophyll.

"No kidding," she says. She doesn't sound too happy.

Ms. Keller shuffles some papers around on her desk, like she can't find something. She glances up, makes sure everybody's still reading.

Then she slips out of the room.

"Looks good," I tell Chlo. Because it does. I don't usually like super-short hair on girls, but it's brown all over now, so I'd have to say she's crossed the line into humanhood.

Chlo makes a face.

"It really does," I tell her, and I'm not sure why I'm trying to convince her I mean it. Maybe because she's going to help me pass English.

"You mean it makes me look like Peter *Pan*."

I start to laugh. But then I realize she's serious.

"That's what Brian said." Chlo turns and looks at me from under her brand-new bangs. They make her eyes look bigger, her lashes longer. "He said it made me look like a boy."

I stare at her. The guy must be blind. It's her *clothes* that make her look like a boy. The *hair* looks great. It looks . . . soft.

Boy, I'd never tell Grace her new haircut sucked. I could tell somebody like Alicia Doggett, easy. Maybe even somebody like Dori.

But no way would I ever be so stupid as to tell my goddamn *girlfriend* her haircut looked bad, for Christ's sake. Now if it was Silver Stanton, I'd shout it off the top of the auditorium. But not my girlfriend. It would hurt her feelings. And it's not like she could glue it back on or anything. "I got to tell you something, Chlo," I say, and for once I tell the absolute truth. "You're too good for that guy. Dump him."

I think about how I'd feel if somebody said something like the Peter Pan comment to Grace.

"*Now*," I tell her. "Today. Pick up the goddamn phone

and dump him. Because I can tell you right now, you're in for a whole load of shit if you don't."

"You can talk," she says. "You're the one calling me Greenland and Chlorophyll."

"I don't call you Greenland anymore," I say. "And I call you Chlo, not Chlorophyll. It's like a nickname. Hell, *you* call *me* Terrell."

"So?"

"So my name's *Trammel*. Colt *Trammel*. Jesus. Haven't you ever been to a high-school baseball game? Don't you read the papers? Do you ever get *out*?"

"Take out your folders," Ms. Keller says, walking back in with her grade book. "I'm checking assignments fifteen through twenty."

"Here's some friendly advice, Chlo," I add, getting out my folder. "Get a life—that's my advice."

I actually have the assignments for Ms. Keller to look at. All finished, too; I copied them from Stu.

So I sit with my open folder, waiting for Ms. Keller to come around with her grade book. Chlo sits too, but she keeps her face down. She really looks depressed all over, with her too-big shirt hanging down almost to her knees.

It pisses me off. Everything's right on track for Grace and me. I'm going to pass all my classes, even if I have to bust a grape to do it. I've got on my favorite shirt in the whole world, which Grace said is her favorite because it makes my eyes look green—which they're not, exactly—and my hair look blond—which it's not, exactly—so it's my favorite shirt, too.

And I don't like the way Chlo's moping around at my lab table, throwing me off balance.

Just because I need her for English, it's like I'm supposed to *do* something now.

Ms. Keller comes by, starts leafing through my folder. I don't look at Chlo again. I can see her sitting there, though, and I can hear the way she doesn't say another word, all through the rest of class.

And all through class, I'm not feeling as great as I was. I've got this tiny, nagging little feeling. Like something's *off*. Like the earth's just a little bit crooked, or the light is not quite right.

By fifth Chlo seems to have worked herself out of her bad mood, thank God. In assistant, we have papers to grade again. Just my luck—when I'm starting to need this time for something besides sleep, Miss A. starts dumping actual work on us.

I slap grades on those papers like I'm dealing cards. Any mistakes'll get caught by whoever gets 'em back, anyway.

I grab some out of Chlo's stack, because she's moving too slow.

Finally Chlo lays the last paper on top of the finished pile. "Okay," she says. She pulls my English book over to her and flips through. "Let's start with 'Ozymandias.'"

Whatever. I bend over a piece of paper, clutching my pencil.

"This is by Percy Shelley," she tells me, and then she reads the poem out loud, slowly, like I'm going to understand it better if she reads it that way. Hah.

> "I met a traveller from an antique land
> Who said: Two vast and trunkless legs of stone
> Stand in the desert. Near them, on the sand,
> Half sunk, a shattered visage lies, whose frown,
> And wrinkled lip, and sneer of cold command,
> Tell that its sculptor well those passions read
> Which yet survive, stamped on these lifeless things,
> The hand that mocked them, and the heart that fed;
> And on the pedestal these words appear:
> 'My name is Ozymandias, king of kings:
> Look on my works, ye Mighty, and despair!'
> Nothing beside remains. Round the decay
> Of that colossal wreck, boundless and bare
> The lone and level sands stretch far away."

She finishes while I'm still copying down the title. It's hard because I'm having to look at it upside down. "Okay," Chlo says. "What do you think this might be about?"

I glance over at her. Is she kidding? "I can't even pronounce it."

She's looking at me through her glasses, not over them. "*Ozy*, like in Ozzy Osborne. *Man*, like in guy. *Dias*, like in . . ." She can't think of anything. "Mandias, like in candy ass," she says triumphantly. "Got it?"

I try to read it off my piece of paper. "Ozzy . . . mandyass."

"Mandyus," she says, which is not the same thing.

Whatever. I don't need to know how to say it, anyway.

She taps her pen on the edge of the table. She's getting that spacey look. "Where do you think this poem takes place?"

I wish she'd stop asking questions. "I'm paying *you* to tell *me*."

She stops tapping. "It takes place in the desert. There's this statue, in the desert."

I write that down, about the desert.

"It's fallen down, so there's just these two legs sticking up. You can't see anything else but the broken-off face, lying half buried in the sand. And nothing else is around for miles and miles."

I write down the part about a broken face, buried.

"And on the pedestal, under what's left of the legs, it says, 'Look on my works, ye Mighty, and despair.'"

I write, "Look on my work," but then I forget what else she said.

"Pretty ironic, huh?"

"Oh yeah," I agree. "Ironic as hell. What came after 'look on my work'?"

"It's in the poem. You don't have to write it down."

I give her a disgusted you-stupid-bitch look. I *do* have to write it down. It'll be like I never heard of it if I don't write it down.

Chlo shuts the book. When she pushes it away from her, I wish to God I could take that look back. I've pissed her off.

"Hey," I tell her, "Chlo. I tend to get a little uptight—"

"What," she interrupts, "do you think *this* place will look like in a thousand years?"

Silence. "I don't know," I say, pretty nicely for me, because I don't want to piss her off any more than I already have.

"You ever been to any place that's fallen down? Or been torn down?"

"Yeah," I say, nice and easy, although a glance at my watch tells me we've only got fifteen more minutes in here.

"What did it make you think of?"

"Look." I'm starting to lose it. "I'm not paying you to fucking converse with me. I'm paying you to get me ready for a test."

"I'm trying to." She's glaring at me. "If you have a problem with my methods, say so now. Don't waste my time."

"Okay, okay. Don't get your panties in a wad."

"And considering what an . . . uptight person you are, I think I'm going to require payment in advance."

"I thought you wanted to figure out the terms later."

"I just figured them out. I want my money."

"Fine," I spit at her. "How much?"

"Fifteen an hour."

"Fifteen? Jesus, I'm not *that* stupid."

"Thirty's the going rate for a private tutor."

"No way!"

"Then take your book back and leave me alone." She shoves the book at me. It slides across the table and hits me in the chest.

I don't know why people helping me makes me such a beast. I'm even worse when Mom tries. And my sister, Cass, God—one time back in fifth grade she was supposed to help me, only I shoved her off the chair next to me, and she jumped up and started pounding me, and we ended up rolling around on the floor. Of course, she was only in third grade, so I won. But at the end I still couldn't do the homework and Mom was mad at me, and Cass sneaked into my room and scratched one of my CDs. Although she denies it to this day.

Chlo's flipping through *her* book now, looking for her place. She's going to zone out if I don't do something.

I reach into my back pocket, pull out my wallet. There's two twenties and a five; I haven't spent much of my allowance yet.

I peel off a twenty and flick it toward her. "Now you *owe* me some time."

She looks at the money like it's dirty. "What about the stuff I told you about Byron and Wordsworth?"

"You didn't talk about those guys for an *hour*. More like five minutes."

"More like *thirty*, you homophobic neanderthal."

I'm getting pretty pissed now. But I'd rather swing by my nuts than ask her what that meant, and I've *got* to pass this test. And I can get more money from my dad anytime.

I pull out the five and send it sliding across the table. Five more—that's all. If she doesn't take it, fuck her.

She doesn't pick it up. Our eyes are locked together. We're like gunfighters, waiting to see who'll draw first.

The bills sit there. And sit there.

And sit there.

"How about," she says, "if I do things my way, and when the bell rings you tell me if today, plus Byron and Wordsworth, is worth twenty-five bucks."

I'm still pissed, but also kind of relieved. There's a way out of this.

I nod.

"So." She settles back in her chair. "This place you went to, that had been torn down. What kind of place was it?"

"I didn't really *go* there, but it's a vacant lot that used to be a baseball field." I can't help it if there's a nasty edge to my voice. "Or not even a field, really. But it was there when I was little."

"Has it changed?"

Duh. "Yeah."

"So I'm guessing there were a lot of kids who played on that field over the years, right?"

"How would I know?"

"Just listen. You used to watch them play on it, right? So picture a kid, a boy like you, playing on this field."

I want to ask why, but I'm trying to be careful. "Okay," I say.

"All right. Let's say this kid was really into baseball for a while, and he was out there every day with his friends. He just loved throwing and catching the ball, and hitting it with the bat—"

174

As opposed to what? Hitting it with a shovel? Chlo obviously isn't a sports fan.

"But let's say he was just an average player—"

"No, say he was really good," I tell her. "Say he turned out to be great at it."

"Okay, he was really great, he was the athletic type. But he got interested in other things, like maybe skate-boarding or—"

"No, I just moved up to kid pitch," I put in.

"Terrell—"

"Trammel."

"Trammel, everyone is *not* like you. People are differ-ent. Another kid, he might not have been good at base-ball. He might have been unathletic and bookish. He might have been scrawny and ugly—"

"Definitely not like me," I point out.

"But let's say you're right, this kid was good, maybe he moved on to bigger and better things, baseball-wise."

"And he was so good at it that he got a scholarship and then went straight to the major leagues."

"Okay, maybe he got into the NFL, or ALA, or what-ever it's called—no, let me finish—and at the same time other kids grew up, gradually stopped using the field too, and eventually it got sold for a parking lot or some-thing. Now, here's the point: For whatever reason, the kid grew older, and the field is gone. And now you're out there looking at where he used to play, where he used to feel the joy of being really good at something, at the place that made him see that he wanted to go and do this baseball thing for the rest of his life." Chlo's getting herself worked up. "But now nobody who drove by would ever know that this kid had found his lifetime desire right there on that spot."

It flashes through my head, then. The vacant lot, the old field.

"What the *fuck*," I blurt, "does this have to do with a desert with a face sticking out of it?"

Chlo's face was starting to get that intense far-off look that Grace's sometimes gets when she's off somewhere in her own mind. But the look fades pretty quick when I say that.

"This poem's about a king, Terr—Trammel. A king who built huge statues of himself. He thought he was such hot shit—rich, very powerful. And thousands of years later, all that's left of him is two broken-off legs and a shattered face, in the middle of a desert."

Why couldn't she just say that in the first place?

"What was it like for the kid, when he was on that field feeling happy and feeling like he'd found his place in the world?" she asks, and she's looking at me in a way Grace never has—angry, and a little sad. "Who knows?

Who cares? And what's left of the place that got him started on his life's path?"

Nothing, I realize. Not a goddamn thing.

"All those feelings, and nothing left behind. What are *you* leaving behind, Trammel? What'll people see, in a thousand years, that you cared about?"

The bell rings. She doesn't get up. She's just looking at me, still angry. Still sad.

And I'm looking at her.

This is too intense. I push my chair back and stand up.

"So," Chlo says, almost lightly. "That's today's session. What's it worth?"

I don't know. I can't think. I didn't write down anything. But I think I might remember the poem. And its title. And I don't want to piss her off.

I lean across the table, and put my hand over the five. "That was worth twenty," I tell her. "And I'm being kind here."

Then I remember I've got one more Romantic poet to go.

"Aw, hell," I say. I let go of the five, and step back. "Take it. Just take it." I grab my book and turn away. After all, I can get money from my dad anytime.

I glance back over my shoulder as I walk out the door.

She's already forgotten me.

She's gathering her stuff together.

• • •

I'm walking down the hall to my locker, and everything looks strange. Distant, like I'm standing above,
looking down. How many years' worth of students have
walked down this hall? Everyone's smiling, talking,
yelling, laughing—but it's all just a low buzz, like it's
already fading into echoes. Already we're all a few steps
closer to the end of our lives.

I'm seeing things like an old man. Who are all these
young people with the short, short lives? It's creepy, it's
sad. It could almost make a guy panic, to see things this
way.

"Hey, Trammel." It's Patrick, beside me. "You hear
some of the juniors are having a kegger this weekend?"

"Yeah," I say, and as soon as I speak, everything shifts
one degree back toward normal. "You guys going?"

"Yeah."

The weird feeling's starting to leave me. "You know
that chick that used to have half-green hair?" I ask
Patrick.

"No. I mean, I've seen her, but I don't know her."

"Stay away from her," I warn him. "She's weird. She's
got these weird ideas."

"Like what?"

"I don't know." The faraway feeling is gone, and now
I'm starting to lose even the sense of what Chlo said.

"She makes you feel old," I tell Patrick, but I can't explain why.

Patrick disappears into the crowd. I'm starting to feel better.

That Chlo. She really can mix people up.

CHAPTER EIGHT

Colt Trammel, That's Who

The next day I'm walking out of biology when I see Grace in front of some lockers not too far from Ms. Keller's room.

She's never in this hall at this time of the morning. What a great picture she makes. She's wearing jeans and a rich brown shirt that buttons up the front. She's got on these boots that make her look long and leggy; she looks like a model, standing there talking to some other girl who is squatting down, getting something out of the bottom of her locker.

I slow down. I don't care if I'm late and my tech ed teacher gets pissed. I'm just happy I'm going to get to talk to Grace for a moment. Even just watching her perks me up. She's the only girl I've ever seen who's really truly beautiful. Everything about her is soft and natural—she's like a butterfly you'd better not close your hand around or you'd crush it.

"He wouldn't do that," I hear Grace saying to the other girl, as I get closer.

"He *did* do that," the girl says, and stands up, holding her books.

It's Silver Stanton.

She sees me, over Grace's shoulder, and gives a nervous little whinny, which makes Grace turn around.

She doesn't look happy. "Colt," she says. "Come here. There's something I want to ask you."

Oh God, I think. Silver told Grace how I felt her up.

Okay. I'm going to play this totally cool.

I force a smile up on my face—my brain's clicking like a machine, trying to line up some way out of this. Grace wasn't even speaking to me when I was all over Silver. It didn't mean anything to me, anyway. It was Silver's idea in the first place.

I stroll right up to them, like I'm not walking onto a minefield.

"Morning, ladies," I say, super gallant. Let *them* feel uncomfortable, not me.

"Hi," Silver says, tossing her hair.

Grace's got her head down. I know that look. She's thinking.

But when she raises her head, she's got this expression I've never seen before. Like she's able to look inside my head. And I'm pretty sure I don't want her in there right now.

"Is it true?" she asks me. "Did you tell Max Gutterson to lock a cat in a freezer?"

It doesn't register for a second. I was expecting the word *Silver*, not *cat*, and it doesn't make any sense.

For just a second, and then I understand.

Oh, God.

The cat. I'd forgotten about the cat. How'd Silver find out about the cat?

"Who told you that?" I don't ask Grace, I ask Silver. Trying to buy some time.

"Alex Simmons," says Silver. "And he got it straight from Max Gutterson."

The hamster/toilet thing doesn't even scratch the surface of how Grace feels about animals. She always insists I carry an old blanket in my trunk, in case we come across a roadkill that's not quite killed yet.

"Alex Simmons," I burst out, "is a fucking idiot."

As soon as it's out, I know I shouldn't have said it. Now I've got two strikes. One for saying the F word in front of Grace. And two because Silver might tell Alex Simmons that I called him an idiot.

"All I want to know," Grace says, and now she looks a little the way I remember the cat did when I opened the freezer door, "is if you did it or not."

My brain's stuck in glue. If I admit I did tell Gutterson that, she's going to hate me. If I say I let the cat *out* of the freezer, Silver'll hunt up Gutterson and tattle—and then I'll really be in deep shit.

For a split second I think, *Just tell the truth*.

But Jesus, it was a while back. And it was a long, complicated truth even when I could remember it.

"Did what?" I ask.

"Tell Max Gutterson to lock a cat in a freezer," Grace says, and her face is getting so stiff, it looks like it's going to crack.

Silver doesn't even bother pretending she's not listening. She's just standing there with her ears pricked up.

Who said I owe anybody any explanations anyway?

"*Colt*," Grace says.

It occurs to me I'm really looking whipped here. Called on the carpet by my girlfriend. "Okay," I say. I'm getting mad, too, now. "Whatever. I did *not* lock the cat in the freezer."

Grace puts one hand on her hip. "But it was your idea, Colt. Wasn't it?"

Her eyes are starting to tear up—it's Death of a Hamster, Part Two. I can't believe this. The stupid cat thing took less than ten minutes. It happened weeks ago. The cat wasn't even hurt.

"No," I tell her.

183

"You are *lying*." The wetness in her eyes is almost to spillover point. She really is about to cry, right here in the hall. Big neon tears, flashing: *My boyfriend's such an asshole!*

"Grace, listen. Forget it—the cat is *fine*. Just trust me on this one, okay?" I say.

"No," Grace says, in this angry, teary voice. "*You* forget it. Forget *everything*.

"Murderer," she adds as she turns away, and gives me this one last look, like I just stepped on something delicate and crushed it.

"Gosh, I didn't mean to get you in trouble," Silver neighs, but I don't even look in her direction.

I just stand there with my arms dangling at my side, watching Grace disappear down the hall, leaving the company of this filthy cat molester.

Okay, so here we go again. If she'd just slow down and let me explain—but no, she's got to jump all over me, not give me time to think.

At lunch I tell Eric and Patrick and Stu that I want to hit some balls. If any of them see that I'm working not to get into a mood, they either don't notice or don't care. They're cool with going down to the field, and that's all that matters.

I toss the ball up, and . . . *Whap!*

Deep right field, over Eric's head. He chugs along after it, tosses it back to me.

I catch it in my bare left hand. It stings, it feels good, it's good to have pain you can put your fingers around.

I toss it up again. *Whap!*

Patrick misses, has to root around for it in the grass by the fence.

It goes like that for what's left of lunch. I don't say where I'm going to hit it, and if any of the guys complain, I don't notice. They're probably panting too much anyway. And when the bell rings, I cram everything in my bag and walk off. I don't wait to see if anybody follows.

It's okay. I'll just let Grace hang for a while. Let her figure out things for once, that she can't keep getting in a wad over some stupid dumb thing. Let her learn that real life isn't a book or a movie, that regular guys don't get their lines written for them.

That just because your boyfriend comes up with the bright idea of freezing a cat doesn't mean he loves you any less.

In assistant, I know I ought to work on English. But I don't feel like it.

I'm tired of being knocked back to square one with Grace.

When Chlo comes in, I'm sitting with my head down, cheek on the table, hands in my lap. I'm looking toward the window. The wood feels cool and hard on my face.

"You look like shit," she says as her backpack *thunk!*s into place.

"So do you," I mumble from the tabletop.

She sits down. I don't look up.

"Anything wrong?"

I don't answer, just turn my face to the tabletop, bang my forehead a couple of times.

When I stop, she asks, "Want to talk about it?"

"No," I say to the table.

Chlo unzips her backpack.

"There was this thing with a cat," I tell her. "My girl-friend's mad at me again."

I hear her taking some stuff out. "Have you tried to talk to her about it?"

"I'm not too quick when it comes to thinking up the right thing to say. You know that."

"Actually, I think you're a little too quick for your own good."

I lay my cheek back on the cool wood.

"So go talk to her," Chlo suggests.

"I can't."

"Write her a note."

"I can't."

"Oh-*kay*." I hear her pull my book over to her. "You ready to take on Keats?"

"No."

"When's your test?"

"I dunno."

I hear her sigh. "Look, if you want to talk to her, talk to her. If you don't, don't. But quit sulking around."

"Look who's talking," I say. "*Peter Pan.*"

"All right. Fine. I'm not saying anything else."

"Good."

"Except this: friendly advice, Trammel. Just tell her how you feel. That's all. If she knows you at all, she'll understand whatever it is you're trying to say."

The sound of a book opening. I'm thinking about how mad Grace gets over nothing. And the way Grace looks at me sometimes, when she forgets to be uptight.

Chlo's about to sail off to la-la land. Even though her body'll still be here.

I lift my head. "Hey Chlo. Can I ask you something?"

She shrugs, leafing through the pages like she's looking for something.

"Was Brian the first guy you ever did it with?"

Chlo actually looks up—from a book! "What business is it of yours?" She sounds like a twenty-foot brick wall.

"None," I say.

"That's right," she says, and goes back to her reading.

I'm still thinking. I know the way Chlo operates. I know I can ask her anything. She may not answer, but she won't spread it around, either. The problem is, I don't know how to ask her what I want to ask her.

I slide down in my chair a little. I pick up one of Chlo's pencils. I start to camouflage the old "Colt" I wrote on the table by making the *C* into a *G*. "They say your first time is pretty important," I comment.

As soon as it's out of my mouth, I'm sorry I said it.

"Oh, yeah? Who was your first?"

"None of your business."

She stares at me for a moment. "You've never done it."

I give a little snort of laughter. "I've done it ways you can't even imagine," I tell her, without looking up.

"Like what?"

"Scuba diving."

I can feel Chlo looking at me. She doesn't ask about scuba diving. Doesn't say anything at all.

Just keeps . . . looking.

I lift my chin and look back. Across the table, right in her face, so I don't appear shifty-eyed.

"It's okay if you've never done it," she says, almost gently. "There's nothing wrong with that."

"Hey," I say, dead serious, but suddenly I'm looking here, there, anywhere but at her. "I've done it. It's great." I focus on the table and start scratching again.

I'm going to make the L into a very large, lopsided A.

"I know you, Trammel. You are *lying*. I can tell. There's nothing wrong with admitting the facts."

"What facts?" If I put a curve on the side of the t, it'll say *GoAd*. Only I'm not sure if that's a word.

"That you," she says, "are one horny lying virgin."

"Yeah?" I leave it at *GoAt*, and lean back in my chair. If I can make Jordan Palmer believe I did the dirty at forty feet, I can make Chlo believe it, too.

"And spare me any details about water depth and oxygen requirements."

Took the words right out of my mouth.

I act like I'm examining my artwork.

"And for your future information, Trammel, *where* isn't as important as *how*," she says, so I know she's decided to let the scuba thing go for the moment. "What matters to the girl is that you take your time and do it right."

"No argument there," I agree. I act like I'm brushing off eraser flecks, though I haven't erased anything.

"Most guys . . ." Chlo pauses—but then she goes on. "Most of the guys I went out with before Bri didn't have a clue. No finesse. I always felt like a melon or something."

"A melon?"

"You know. Like your breasts? Just squeeze, squeeze, squeeze."

I'm wondering what else there is to do to breasts. I'm wondering if the girls I've been out with thought I was some kind of spaz, because all I did was squeeze.

I don't say anything, though, because I don't want to lose my credibility with Chlo. If I have any left.

I just get a firm hold on my pencil and add the word *me*. It'll say "GoAt me," and everybody'll think there's a new obscene saying they never heard of.

Chlo bends her head over her book again. We work in silence for a while.

"You know," she says suddenly, "when you were asking about the picture in my head?"

"Huh?"

"The picture. Remember, we were talking about Byron and 'She Walks in Beauty'?"

Oh. "Yeah."

"The picture I get is of the first time Brian and I made love."

I drop my pencil.

Chlo doesn't notice. The look on her face is a little frightening. Not dreamy. Her eyes are narrowed a little. She looks . . . *hungry*. "It was in his room. The lights were out, and the moonlight came in the window. He was all silver and shadows. I wrote a poem about it."

"A poem," I echo. The news is flashing, all through my body—This Girl Loves Sex.

"It was like the tide coming in and going out."

Across the table from me I can't see any body parts that I don't normally see. But with her hair cut short, I can see the line of her neck, I can see tiny earrings I never noticed before, made of the same milky stone as her ring.

"What kind of earrings are those?" I ask, to get her talking about something else.

"What?"

"Your earrings."

"Oh. Opals."

I nod. I wonder if Brian gave her the earrings. I wonder if Brian kissed her neck, right there where her hairline swoops down behind her ear.

Probably. He probably did everything. Except squeeze.

I duck under the table, looking for my pencil. By the time I come back up, Chlo's deep in her book again.

I don't write again. I just sit there, hoping to God I haven't made an asshole out of myself with every girl I ever touched.

Don't squeeze. I file it away, thinking about Grace. They don't like to be squeezed.

Over the next few days I pick up the phone exactly three times. Even dial half Grace's number once.

But I don't call her. Don't speak to her at all. It's a record. I've never lasted this long before without doing something stupid that I was sorry for later.

I keep saying to myself, Who's the one girls say is cute? Who's the one with messages on his answering machine all the time? Who's the one with love notes left on his windshield after games last year?

Colt Trammel, I remind myself. That's who.

WEEK FIVE

CHAPTER NINE

He Died Slowly, Coughing Up Blood

On Thursday I'm coming in from lunch. I know that Grace is on her way to biology, so I'm going to be a good boy again today and not go anywhere near the science hall.

Only it turns out that what I know is dead wrong.

I see her as I'm turning the corner to head down the English hall. Grace and . . .

Jordan Palmer?

My feet slow and stop. People brush by me, but I'm stuck now, drilled to the floor by the sight of them.

Jordan Palmer!

She's leaning back against the wall by his locker. They are very close. Jordan is leaning over her, braced by one hand on the wall, and their faces are just inches apart while they're talking and smiling at each other.

Or actually, Jordan's talking. Grace is listening.

Really listening. She's looking at him like she's got to memorize every bit of his face.

If you've never experienced something like this situation, I'll tell you how it feels. You wish a giant meteor would shoot from the sky and turn the earth backward for a few seconds and rewind time so that you could change everything that you just saw. And since that's not possible, you wish the giant meteor would cut off the top of your head and take away the memory of what you just saw.

And since that's not possible, you just wish the giant meteor, or anything else heavy like an iron or a baseball bat, would fall and squash you like a bug on the spot.

Palmer acts like he doesn't even notice he's got the undivided attention of the most beautiful girl in the sophomore class. He's used to that kind of thing.

He's talking—whispering, looks like, and whatever it is he's saying, she's looking straight up into his eyes like she's the only girl he's ever talked to this way. Like she really believes he sees only her. Like she's not just one more in the long line of girls that Palmer's leaned over and whispered the right words to.

My Grace isn't that stupid. To believe that Palmer is anything but some horny senior who's turned on the charm. No way.

Grace is an intelligent girl. A lot smarter than me. I know that. I know her.

I know her.

I keep putting one foot in front of the other. I'm breathing hard through my nose, fighting this urge to go back and look down the hall to see if they're still together, the same way I've seen girls fight not to peek through covered eyes during the worst part of a horror movie.

Whack me in the head with that hammer again, please. It didn't hurt enough the first time.

I'm fighting it all the way down the hall. I know it's loud in here as usual, but inside my head it's quiet.

Too quiet.

Sinking-in quiet.

"Ready to try some Keats?" Chlo says. She's got her hand on her book.

"No."

"He's not so bad. And remember, you ended up liking Shelley."

"Not his poems. His poems suck." The reason I liked Shelley is that he was this atheist who got kicked out of school and ran off with jailbait, so his wife drowned herself and then he drowned, and his new wife took his heart and put it in a box.

"Would you rather skip it today? I take it you're still having girlfriend troubles," she adds.

I *would* rather skip it. But I shrug and say, "Go ahead and read it," because I don't want to hear or talk about or admit to girlfriend troubles.

She starts "Ode on a Grecian Urn," out loud like she always does.

> *"Thou still unravish'd bride of quietness,*
> *Thou foster-child of silence and slow time,*
> *Sylvan historian, who canst thus express*
> *A flowery tale more sweetly than our rhyme:*
> *What leaf-fringed legend haunts about thy shape*
> *Of deities or mortals, or of both,*
> *In Tempe or the dales or Arcady?*
> *What men or gods are these? What maidens loth?*
> *What mad pursuit? What struggle to escape?*
> *What pipes and timbrels? What wild ecstasy?—"*

"What crap," I interrupt. "This is torture."

"It's a little difficult."

"You think I can pass without knowing this one?"

"I don't know. It's up to you whether you want to try."

"The words are too big. I don't know what they mean by themselves, much less together."

"Which ones?"

I scan the page. "All of them. Unravish'd. Syl-van. Historian—no, wait, I know what that is. *Freengd—*"

"Fringed," she says, with a j. "Like tassels. You know?"

"Dytees," I go on, clenching my jaw. I hate it when people correct me.

"Deities. That means gods."

"*Tempe,*" I say, triumphant. "Ha. I know that. That's where the Cardinals play."

"It's a valley in Greece, Trammel. See the footnote?"

I don't want to see the goddamn footnote. "This," I announce, shutting the book, "is bullshit."

"Why don't we trying breaking it down?"

"It'll just be broken-down bullshit."

"Does it help to know that it's about a vase?"

Today sucks so bad. And I look at the closed book, with that stupid poem inside, and all of a sudden it's like there's a sizzling filling my lungs. Every page is written in a foreign language that everybody understands but me. It's like some club, and people like Jordan Palmer and Grace were born into it, while I've been shut out from day number one. Without even a *chance* to get in.

And it's not fair that I get to be stupid and at the same time know how stupid I am. It seems like if you're stupid, you shouldn't have to know it.

"The writer," Chlo continues, "is looking at this old vase with pictures—"

"How do you *get* that?" I burst out—I feel like I'm going to burst a vein. "Is it in some kind of code? Jesus, there wasn't a thing in there about a fucking vase."

"It's in the title. An urn is a vase."

I slap the book off the table. *Bang!* It hits the cabinets—Chlo flinches—and then, with a fluttering of pages, it falls.

"This is *useless*. You don't know how hard I work," I tell her, and I don't bother to keep my voice down. "I work my ass off to learn one tenth of the stuff everybody else was born knowing."

"Trammel, everybody has to study."

"Yeah?" I lean forward, jabbing the air in front of her face with my finger. "I'll bet you never had to study all these words. I'll bet you already knew them all. I'll bet you never had to study *urn!*"

She's looking over the table at me, wide-eyed.

And then her mouth quivers.

"Go ahead," I tell her, as she starts laughing. "I know it's funny. It's real funny, that I've got a defective brain."

I stand up, kick my chair out of the way, and head for the door.

"Trammel," says Chlo. "Hey. Think of it like baseball."

I stop, hand on the doorknob.

"You're in baseball, right? You don't go straight to the stadium and walk onto the field and start playing right away, do you? No, you get to the park early and make sure you warm up real good. You do your windmills and your back bends."

I don't know what the hell she's talking about.

"And if you think you might be getting into a losing streak, you don't stop doing all those warmups, do you? No, you take even *more* care. You do the extra jumping jacks, you do the extra toe touches."

Toe touches? I can't help it, I make a face—not to where Chlo could see, but at the door. "You don't know shit about baseball, do you?"

"No. I'm stupid about baseball. Everybody's stupid about something."

I let go of the doorknob. My hand drops down to my side.

"So you going to stand there? Because I've got a book I could be reading."

I don't say anything. I just turn around and come back. I pick up my English book, but I don't open it, just toss it on the table in front of Chlo.

My chair fell over; I pick it up, too, but I turn it around and straddle the seat facing the chair back, to show that I'm done reading and writing and thinking today.

"Okay, Chlo," I tell her. "Warm me up. Warm me up real good."

She gives me an over-the-glasses look, but I keep my face straight.

So she tells me about Keats, who loved this one woman, Fanny Brawne, all his life, and how he died slowly, coughing up blood, so that he knew he was going to die. And how he realized that this vase with pictures on it would outlast him, and how maybe he got comfort from the fact that something beautiful could last forever.

"Fanny?" I blurt. "Isn't that another word for—"

"I think it's short for Frances."

"Fanny. God. Why didn't they just name her Assy? Or Butty. No, Butthilda! 'Oh, Butthilda,'" I say, in the same slow voice Chlo uses for reading this shit, "'thou dost freeng thy dytees in Tempe.'"

Chlo actually cracks a smile. Her teeth are straight, like someone who's had braces. "Trammel, you're a case."

"Yeah, I'm pretty hopeless," I agree—but then I realize it's true. I've been smiling, too, but now the smile dies. "And I'm tired of English."

"I know." She doesn't say whether she knows I'm hopeless or I'm tired. Both, probably.

I reach around, pull out my wallet. Start digging in for her fifteen bucks.

"You going to remember any of this?" she asks.

"No."

"Then save it."

"I don't mind, Chlo." I look at her, she's just watching me, arms folded.

"Save it."

I shrug and stuff the wallet back in my pocket. I get

comfortable, rest my arms on the chair back in front of me, because it's probably a few minutes till the bell. I'm expecting Chlo to open up her book and disappear.

She doesn't—she just sits there, arms still folded, like she's expecting me to say something.

She thinks this is a real conversation.

I drop my chin down onto my arms. It's one of those moments like when you're dropping a girl off at her front door on a first date. It's that pause when you don't know whether to say good-bye, or start talking again, or just kiss her. Any one of them could be wrong.

"Your boyfriend okay with your hair now?" I ask.

"Yeah. He said he was sorry. I was just pissed."

"You didn't seem pissed. You seemed sad."

"That too."

"If he said he's sorry, maybe you don't have to dump him after all. Maybe he just blurted the Peter Pan thing out without thinking about it."

"Probably."

"I know, because I do that kind of stuff. Blurting."

"I noticed."

"You really do look good, you know. Your hair. Like that."

"Thanks."

The bell rings. Thank God. Now I don't have to figure out what to say next.

• • •

Now it's athletics and I'm standing near the sit-up board, getting ready to do some abs.

Or really, I'm thinking.

Palmer's in the smart classes. That doesn't mean much. Most of the people in the smart classes are in there just because they've always been in there. That's the way it is; ever since I was a little tyke trying to figure out p, q, b, and d, the smart people have been in the smart classes. But most of them aren't into the intellectual stuff like Grace is. Most of them don't even like to read. I know, because she complains about them sometimes.

On the other hand, if Jordan's even a little into the intellectual stuff, that's more than me.

I watch Palmer out of the corner of my eye. "Bottom line: you got to go with whoever's making the plays," he's saying to Gutterson.

I sit on the slanted board. "Hey Palmer," I burst out "You into poetry?"

Palmer stops talking and turns to stare at me. "Poetry? No. Why?"

"Just wondering." Gutterson's staring at me too. I know my face is getting red.

"Why were you wondering?"

I loosen one of my weight-lifting gloves, act like I'm

pulling it tighter. "Um." Think fast. "I was thinking if writing a poem to a girl might help me get laid." Ooh, that's just great, Colt, you dumb fuck. Act like some virgin asking the pro for advice.

"Oh." Palmer grins. "Sure. Just give me a second. Let me think." He stares at the ground for a moment, like he's thinking. Just a moment, then his head pops back up and he's got this sincere look. "How about this:

"Violets are blue,
Roses are red,
I'm desperate and horny—
Willya give me some head?"

Palmer and Gutterson about fall over, laughing.

I'm not laughing. The scary thing is how fast he came up with it. This guy is smart. Evil and smart. That's a bad combination.

"Big help, Palmer," I tell him, sitting on the board. I slide one foot under the bar. "Thanks a lot."

They go on about their business, and I go about mine. But when it's time to quit, when I'm putting up my weights and Gutterson heads out to the locker room, Palmer walks over to where I'm putting the weights back on the rack, and says in a low voice, "Hey, Trammel." And when I look up, he says, "Try this:

'Gather ye rosebuds while ye may, / Old time is still a-flying.' Short but sweet. It might be in your English book. 'To the Virgins, to Make Much of Time,' by Robert Herrick."

"Oh. Yeah. That sounds good. Thanks."

"No problem, Trammel my boy. Good luck to you."

He walks out, and all I can think is: Holy shit.

CHAPTER TEN

No Matter How Hard You Try

I see Grace the next day.

I'm sure it's her. I'm heading to fifth period from my locker, and down the hall, among all the other heads bobbing along, I see a blond one, one I'd know anywhere.

Something inside slips out of gear—I've got to make everything right, that's all, just make everything back the way it was.

I tell myself it's going to be okay. Even though with each step a little more panic overtakes me.

"Hey," I call. She doesn't hear me, doesn't stop, and as I shoulder other people aside to catch up to her, my heartbeat revs up so much, I think my voice is going to come out as a high-speed stutter. Inside I'm shouting at myself: Moron, don't you crawl!

"Grace, I want to talk." She glances at me—and just

keeps walking. I have to hustle to keep up. "I just wanted to tell you I'm sorry about everything." Now that I've started, I'm going to keep going till she says she missed me and she's not mad anymore. "I guess it *was* my idea to put the cat in the freezer. But I was just joking, so when Gutterson really did it, I went back and got it out. It's not dead—it's alive. It's still around some-where. I've seen it. Do you believe me?"

"I don't know," she says offhand, not even slowing down. "It doesn't matter."

"Yes, it does." My voice sounds faraway to me, even though I'm right there.

"There's nothing I can do about it one way or the other," she says, shrugging. "All I know is something good came out of it. My eyes have been opened."

"The cat is *fine*, Grace."

She looks annoyed. "Come over here, Colt. Let's get this over with." I follow her over out of traffic, closer to a wall where there's no lockers. When she gets there, when she turns to face me, I get a chill.

She's looking up at me the way the kid in the movie looked at Old Yeller right before he shot him.

Or maybe not. The kid who shot Old Yeller at least was sad about it.

"I'm never going to go out with you again, Colt," Grace says. "I don't even want to see you. We have absolutely no rapport."

Rapport? "Jesus." I can't be bothered trying to keep things clean now. "Will you quit throwing *words* at everything?"

"I'm not even going to try to discuss this with you if you use that kind of language."

Deep breath. I nod: Agreed. No bad words, not even if those are the only words that are in my head.

"Let me see if I can put this a way you'll understand: We have no . . . *connection*."

"You got to *make* a connection, Grace. You can't just *talk*." She frowns, which gives me a chance to jump right in. "We *do* have a—a—we belong together, okay? I told the truth that time when you let me touch—that time in the car. About how I feel—I love you, Grace. Even though I'm not anywhere near the kind of guy I should be, at least I'm trying. It's all right if you don't believe me. I don't blame you. But I want to work things out. And I don't know about connections, but I do know one thing." I take a deep breath. "There isn't anybody but you. For me, I mean. I don't ever want to be with anybody but you."

"It just doesn't work."

"It does. It will. I'm going to try harder."

"It doesn't matter how hard you try."

"Don't say that. It *does* matter." I say it firmly, to show her how right I am. "Look, do you think it's easy, telling you this? You think it's easy to tell you I love you? The last time you didn't speak to me for two days." On the word *days* my voice cracks, just a little. "I'm not asking you to say you love me back. I'm not asking you to do anything at all. All I'm asking is for us go back to the way we were and let me try again."

"I'm sorry, Colt. I'm with someone else now."

All my insides start slithering down into the pit of my gut. My Grace, with her soft hair and her soft lips and her green eyes.

"You can't go out with Jordan Palmer," I say desperately. "He's a jerk. He's screwed about a million different girls. He cheated on his girlfriend with her best friend. He even videotaped—"

"That's a lie!"

"It's true. And he talks about whoever he's screwed. He doesn't always name names, but he always tells the de—"

"Like you don't?"

"—tails. What?"

"Jordan told me how you slept with that girl in the Bahamas this summer. Someone you didn't even know."

Okay, now, sometimes I'm not too bright. Sometimes I don't hear things too clearly the first time.

"What?" I say again.

"I see it on your face; don't even bother trying to deny it. I made myself believe you about a lot of stuff—I was stupid enough to give you the benefit of the doubt. So don't go telling me how we have to work at a connection. Or a bunch of garbage about how you've always loved me. Jordan"—she pauses over his name like it's a drop of honey—"doesn't have to lie. He doesn't have to pretend. The connection is *there*. We didn't force it. It's not something we had to *work* at. It just happened. It was meant to be. Which is not something I could explain to you, Colton Trammel. How everything about two people can just . . . just . . . *click*."

"You do not click with Palmer. He just makes you think you do. No, don't say anything. Will you stop talking for just one second and listen to me? Just listen to me, will you?"

She crosses her arms and glares up at me. Okay, Colt, let's hear your words of wisdom.

Of course my brain goes completely blank.

She's standing there and I'm standing there, and all I can think is that she believes Palmer is like one of those guys in those stupid films she likes, Boy meets Girl, click click click, and the very next moment they're naked and—

"Oh my God," I burst out. "Please tell me you didn't let him fuck you!"

Grace's mouth is an open *O* of shock. Then her face closes up. "I should have known you'd put it that way. You're disgusting."

"Jesus, you just went out with me a *week* ago!"

She's looking at me like I've turned into a maggot. "There is a world of difference between . . . what you said, and making love. What you said—it's demeaning. It's nasty. You're so shallow, Colt. You're a shallow little boy. You'll never understand that two people can have things in common; deep, beautiful things. Yes, like the human body—but you'll never understand that there's more to it than that. Books and poetry and wondering about—well, about life. About ideas. Like whether there's order in the universe, or what people are really like on the inside, or the true meaning behind a piece of art."

She let him fuck her! My head feels like it's going to explode. I'm a lot bigger than she is. I could hurt her if I wanted. I could scare her, too, scare her into crying and make her say she lied and she didn't mean it.

I'd almost like to see her cry, right now.

"Face it, Colt. You aren't capable of a relationship that has any kind of depth to it."

She whirls around and walks off. The bell rings, but all I hear is this tremendous sucking sound as Grace Garcetti removes herself from my life.

● ● ●

Down at the end of the hall I shove the heavy bathroom door open. I wish I could stay in here until the
school empties out. The room stinks of bleach and
cleanser and old urine. It's brighter in here than the
hallway, because of the lights and the windows. A whole
row of windows, up above the sinks and the mirrors.

I don't really need to go. I figure I'll wash my hands,
just to prove I belong in here. I step over to a sink and
turn on the water.

I take a good look at myself in the mirror while I'm
washing my hands. Hair looks good, like always. Face
looks okay, not upset, not mad. It's a little pale, maybe,
but nothing that advertises the whole story: This is a guy
whose life has cracked open beneath his feet.

"Trammel, you stupid bastard," I tell the guy in the
mirror.

The guy in the mirror doesn't say anything.

"Look," I tell him, "I just, you know." I want to explain
something, but I'm not sure what it is. Something about
myself, I guess. But I can't, because like I said I don't
know what it is.

I take my time scrubbing my hands. Then I bend over,
splash some water on my face. But when I shut my eyes
to keep the water out, pictures rise up on the back of my
eyelids.

Where were they when they did it? Did she go home with him? Did she touch him? Did she like it?

Did she make any sounds?

God—the sounds Grace used to make with me! The soft sounds; her lips touching my lips, the way her breath got deeper when I touched her—most of the time through her shirt.

Through her shirt. Jesus.

I brace my palms on the cold, hard rim for a second. I stare down into the sink. In that bright bathroom that stinks of bleach and urine, I think how I gave my heart away to somebody who never wanted it.

And not just once—I gave it to her over and over again, every day, every time I saw her, every time I thought of her, like a dog panting and begging and hoping for just one tiny pat on the head, I gave my whole heart every single day.

There's no paper towels in here, just blow dryers. So I pull my shirttail up and dry my face on that. When I look up again at the guy in the mirror, his eyes are a little red rimmed.

It's so unfair. I've wanted her since seventh grade. Four years I worked to get her. I tried so fucking hard to be whatever it was she wanted.

And all Palmer had to do was just *be*.

I brace my palms on the edge of the sink again and

bow my head, like I'm praying. Only instead I squeeze my eyes shut and tell myself what an asshole I've been.

You're an asshole, Colt Trammel. I tell myself that over and over, hoping the edge will wear off the idea.

Big surprise: It never does. And when I walk out of the bathroom and head toward fifth period, there's a big black hole where my heart used to be.

I want to go home, to creep out of the building, into my car, speed home to go to my room and be alone.

But the only thing that's ever between a guy and total humiliation is *pride*. I've got to act like it doesn't matter.

Hell, it *doesn't* matter. It's just some chick. Who cares?

That's what I tell myself.

I get into assistant somehow and I don't have my English book—maybe it's in my locker, maybe it's on the floor in the hall somewhere—and Chlo's already there, but I don't look at her or say anything. She doesn't say anything either.

I sit down and I keep my head turned, like I'm looking out the window. I don't figure she's stupid enough to try to talk to me. Chlo will see that I'm not in the mood to hear anything today.

She doesn't say a word, but after a few moments she gets her stuff out and goes into the same routine she had before the Romantic poets turned up. Reading. Marking stuff with her pencil.

I put my head down, like I used to do back before my heart got broken.

We sit like that for a while. Her reading and marking. Me trying not to think. Especially not about how I'm supposed to go to sixth period, how I'm supposed to get all the way through that last class in the same weight room as old Pepe LePew Palmer in all his stupid handsome seniorness and his poems and his discussing who won't put out and who will.

The door that leads to Miss. A.'s classroom opens, and I hear Miss. A. come in. "Would you two collate and staple these pages into packets? The pages are numbered, one through seven."

I don't even bother to lift my head.

"Sure," says Chlo. I hear Miss. A.'s heels *pock-pock-pock* back into the other room while Chlo shuts her books and piles them up. Then for a long time, all I hear is the *swish, swish, swish* of paper as Chlo arranges the papers into packets.

"So, Trammel," Chlo asks after a long time. "You okay?"

"Yeah," I'm hidden inside the circle of my arms. And then, I don't know why, I ask, "You?"

"*I'm* fine."

Swish, swish, swish.

"Chin up, Trammel," she says. "Whatever it is, this day is almost over."

"*Almost.* God." I groan and raise my head. My brain feels like it's eating itself from the inside out.

Chlo's got about half the packets done, crisscrossed in a stack.

Aw, fuck it. Working—anything—is better than sitting here *thinking.* "Gimme the stapler and I'll help," I mutter.

"It's not in here. You'll have to get it from Miss. A."

So I get up and trudge into Miss. A.'s classroom to get the stapler.

"Alicia's got it out in the hall," Miss. A. says. "Go check; she's probably done with it."

I go out in the hall, and old Doghead is standing on a chair in front of an open display case, one of those flat ones for posting announcements and lists and that kind of shit. When I walk over, I see my reflection in the glass, and my face has this half smile, half smirk on it, which is weird because I don't feel like I'm smirking. What I feel like is I'm standing on the beach, and the tide is coming in, washing the sand out from under my feet, and no matter how much it knocks me off balance, I've got to look like I'm still standing straight.

Doghead is still using the stapler; she's fastening a

sheet of paper to the cork board inside the case.

"I need the stapler," I tell Alicia. She staples another corner, and I wait for her to finish.

But after the last corner is stapled, Alicia just places the stapler sideways and starts going around the edges of the paper, as if she's got all the time in the world and nobody's waiting.

"Come on," I add. "Hurry up."

"*Please,*" says Alicia, without looking at me. She smoothes the paper with her hand and staples it again.

Very slowly.

Puh-dunk.

Please? She wants me to say "please" to her? I wasn't rude. I didn't call her any names. I'm not asking for any personal favors. I'm trying to do a job for Miss A.

A tiny little spot inside starts burning.

"Give me the fucking stapler," I tell Alicia.

Alicia carefully places the stapler against another edge of the paper and pushes it down. *Puh-dunk*! Then she stops.

The hall is suddenly quiet and still, but even though Alicia's stopped stapling, she doesn't turn and acknowledge me, she just stands there staring at the cork board, breathing hard through her nose.

"Stape-ler," I say the words very slowly. "Give. Me. The. Fuck-ing. Stapler. Doghead."

At the word *Doghead* Alicia turns to me, and I see her pale face, and her eyes burning at me from behind her glasses, and then her hand's coming at me and the open stapler hits me in the forehead.

There's this sick muffled sound, *pa-chung!*—it feels like she punched a hole in my skull—and my head pops back. I hear myself give a gasping little grunt. Alicia's hand pulls back and then I'm bent over in pain, trying to cover my forehead without actually touching it, because there are now two metal prongs sticking into my brain.

"Oh my God," I hear myself moan.

"Don't talk to me like that," Alicia's trembly voice says from above. "Don't ever talk to me like that again."

"Shit. Shit." I squinch up my eyes to keep them from leaking tears of pain right there in front of Alicia and anybody who walks by.

I hear Alicia get down off the chair and she walks away, the psycho, and I kind of turn to the wall so nobody can see, and I'm thinking I've got to get to the bathroom so nobody finds out what just happened.

"There you are." It's Chlo's voice, annoyed. "I figured you'd ditched—what's wrong?"

"Nothing!" I'm all bent over, covering my eyes too now, so Chlo can't see whether I'm crying or not, because I'm not even sure whether I am. "Go away!"

"What is it? What happened? Hey. Are you okay?"

"Fuck no, I'm not okay!" I roar through my hands. "That psycho bitch just stapled me in the head!"

Silence.

"Oh my God," Chlo says, "you've got to go to the nurse."

"No!"

"You might have a concussion. You might need stitches." I feel a hand on my arm. "I'll walk you down."

"No. I just need to go in the bathroom for a minute, that's all."

"If you don't come with me, I'm going to get Miss A. right now and tell her what happened. And she'll tell Coach Kline, you know she will."

"All right! Fuck. All right. But first, swear you won't say anything. Let me do all the talking." Stapled in the head by Alicia Doggett. Good God. I'd never hear the end of it.

She promises, and so, finally, keeping my hand over my staple and my body bent over like Igor, I let Chlo lead me away.

Now I'm sitting on the white cot in the nurse's office, waiting for the nurse to come back from wherever she is—because wherever that is, it's not here where she's supposed to be. Chlo stands next to me, but I don't want her to see my face so I'm sitting all bent over with my hands cupped around my forehead, and all I can see of her is her shoes. My eyes are dry now, but my nose is a little runny. My head has died down to a dull throb. There's still a staple in there somewhere, though.

Chlo doesn't say anything—she's just standing there.

Because there's nothing else to look at, I stare at her shoes. Today they're black leather. Her jeans cover most of them, so I can't tell if she's wearing socks.

She's so quiet, I can hear what she's thinking. She's thinking I probably did something to Alicia, to deserve this stapling.

"It wasn't my fault," I tell Chlo. "I just went out to get the stapler, and she got mad because I wouldn't say '*please*.'"

At that, Chlo clears her throat. "When I came looking for you," she says, and her voice is a little shaky, "she was just walking into the classroom, like nothing had happened."

"She belongs in a mental institution."

"You need to tell somebody what happened."

"No!"

"Why not?"

"God! Why don't you leave?" I tell her. "Why don't you go back to class?" There's a drip forming inside my left nostril, and I sniff without thinking. Then I realize how stupid it sounded, and I wish I'd just let it run down my lip.

Chlo's quiet for a minute. When she speaks, she doesn't sound sorry for me, thank God. She just sounds normal. "You were already having a bad day, huh, Trammel?"

"No shit."

"I've noticed that when you have a bad day, everybody around you has to have one, too."

"I didn't do anything to her! I asked her for the stapler, and she hit me with it."

"And that's all?"

"Well, I guess I might have told her instead of asked her. But that's pretty much it."

"Ah." She's quiet a moment, maybe out of respect for my mood, and for my head. "What are you going to tell the nurse?"

"I don't know. That I fell on a stapler."

"You *fell* on it?"

"Yeah, so what?"

"Don't you think—"

"No. So just shut up. Please."

After a few more moments, Chlo's voice sounds above me. "Hey. Trammel. You know I like you okay, don't you?"

"No," I say. Because I don't.

"Well, I do. You're not exactly in the comfort zone, but

you're real. That's more than most people."

My nose is about to drip again. This time I do the smart thing and use my sleeve.

"You hear me?"

"Yeah," I say. She's a pain in the ass, standing here watching me sniff like a moron.

She stays with me till the nurse comes in. I watch her black leather shoes walk away. Don't ask me why, looking at the empty floor where her feet used to be, I feel like some of the air's gone out of me, like an old basketball.

"What have we here?" the nurse asks. Her shoes are tan and flat, with little tassles on them.

"I fell on a stapler," I tell her.

The nurse makes me put my hands down and look at her, and then she rips the staple out of my head. At least that's what it feels like. Only all I end up with is a Band-Aid, no stitches, no trip to the ER. Just a Band-Aid.

And then comes the one single good thing out of the whole day, the only good part of the uprising of Alicia Doggett: I get a pass out of athletics, a note sent to Coach telling why I couldn't participate today.

CHAPTER ELEVEN

Not Quite the End

Driving home, I pull a baseball cap out from under my seat and put it on—gently—to hide the Band-Aid. Then I turn the radio up loud. Real loud. The dashboard is shuddering. At the intersection of University and Berry I can see an old lady in the next car glaring at me, even though all my windows are rolled up.

I don't care. I'm alone. All alone. With a Band-Aid on my head. And my girlfriend—my *ex*-girlfriend—slept with another guy. I've been waiting and begging, holding back, trying to be a good boy . . .

It hits me like a flash: Now I have no reason not to go get laid as quickly as possible.

I see it now: Unloading my virginity is the only thing in the world that could possibly make me feel better right now.

Dori!

I think about it some more as I drive. I'm actually prepared, for a change, and have been for a while. I've been carrying a condom in my wallet for months now. In my closet I've got a whole box of lubricated ribbed I bought at Albertson's earlier in the year. Of course, I didn't know they were lubricated and ribbed till I got home and pulled them out of the bag along with the Dr. Scholl foot pads, Tylenol, hair spray, and Sinutab Non-drying Allergy Geltabs I bought, because at the last minute I couldn't face going up to the checkout lady and tossing one lone box of condoms on the revolving counter. I thought I could, but I couldn't.

I think about that rubber in my wallet, not like I'm deciding whether to go have sex for the first time, but more like I'm deciding whether to get fries to go with my burger.

I believe I will have the fries today.

I've perked up just the tiniest bit now. By the time I get to Dori's house, when I'm pulling up in front of the cracked curb, the saggy screen door and aluminum foil in the windows to keep out the sun, I don't even care that I could for sure do better than this.

On the way across the yard I catch myself pulling the bill of my baseball cap around to the front, like I always do when I'm about to go to Grace's house, because it looks better to parents. But then I tell myself that this is just Dori and who cares, so I turn my cap around to the back again just as I'm stepping onto the flat porch slab.

I raise my hand to knock on the wood frame of the screen door, but Dori must have seen me drive up, because the door opens before I can bring my hand down. She's got her hair parted down the middle and pulled back in a ponytail, but a lot of it's come loose and there's plenty of curls around her face.

"Colt!" She's surprised, but happy to see me. I know, because she's smiling, even while she looks concerned. "What happened to your forehead?"

I guess the Band-Aid shows. I shrug. Which is not like me. It's as if every last smart-ass comment and lie leaked out, and there's not any left.

Which is okay. I just want to get laid, you know. Not talk.

She pushes open the screen door to let me in. "Your dad home?" I ask her, just to check, as I step into the living room.

"No." She peers up at me. "Everything okay?"

"Yeah. I was in the neighborhood, thought I'd drop by."

"Oh, that's nice. You want a Coke?"

"No thanks." She leads me into her living room. We both sit on the couch. She's got on jeans and a tiny little top. Her lips are the best part about her face, full and pouty.

She doesn't say anything, just smiles at me. Even though the couch is very soft and comfortable, I can't seem to settle into a position. Finally I sit forward on the edge. There's a spindly-legged coffee table in front of us, with pieces of patterned paper spread out over it. It looks like she tore the sheets out of a wallpaper sample book. "You still picking out wallpaper?" I ask.

"Yeah." She slides off the couch, onto her knees in front of the coffee table. "See my samples?" she asks. Her feet are bare. "Which do you like best?" She puckers her brow a little and starts patting and pushing the papers like they're old friends.

"They all look pretty good." I'm thinking how they say you shouldn't keep a condom too long in your wallet, and I'm wondering how long is too long.

She's frowning over the papers. A strand of dark hair is caught in the corner of her mouth; she pulls it out. Her hair is dark, so dark that her scalp is a white line where the part is.

It's actually kind of delicate, that white line—as if she's a real *person* who saves up money to decorate her room, and wonders which is prettier, vines or shells?

So I look straight ahead. But when I do that, I can't help but focus on the cheesy kitchen curtains through the doorway. They've got smiling teapots printed all over them.

I shut my eyes for a moment. I don't want there to be anything in my mind but the fact that I'm about to get laid.

Dori doesn't notice anything's different about me— well, besides the Band-Aid. When I open my eyes again, she's still kneeling on the floor, happy with her wall-paper squares. Behind her, the tiny TV in the corner has a rabbit-ear antenna with a coathanger duct-taped to it.

I try not to think. It's hard, though. There's something about that TV. And that white line of skin. About those stupid curtains—they're the kind of thing somebody would sew themselves, if they were trying to make this place look cheery and decent but they didn't know how.

Suddenly I'm feeling funny. I know what I want. But it's tied up with all this other stuff that I've never really thought about.

And don't want to.

"Maybe I ought to go," I tell Dori. But I don't move.

"You just got here. We haven't had a chance to talk." She bends to look past me at the clock, which puts her shoulder inches away from my knee, and I can see right down her shirt, from her neck almost to her nipples.

No bra.

Grace and Palmer; Palmer and Grace. For all these months, she's pushed *my* hands away.

Dori sits up again, which makes her breasts bob slightly, like two balloons. "I guess Jordan's doing okay?" she asks, smiling down at the wallpaper squares.

"Oh yeah," I tell her, low and shaky. "Jordan's doing just fine."

Dori looks up at me. Her smile fades a little. "Is something wrong?"

I don't answer.

My head's still throbbing, but not only from the staple. Grace and Palmer, Palmer and Grace.

There's nothing I can *do*. She picked him, that's all. Not me. Palmer. His stupid smile, his goddamn talk about who moans, who gives head.

I lift my hand, and I'm surprised to see it's trembling a little.

Dori grows very, very still. She freezes as my hand reaches toward her. She lets me do it; she doesn't argue, doesn't move a muscle, just watches my hand slip down into her shirt.

I'm hardly breathing; we both watch my hand as it does its thing.

Okay. Things are getting back to order; I feel like I'm really in control for the first time today.

I realize I've been holding my breath, and when I let it out, I glance at Dori's face again.

She's not smiling anymore. She's not looking at my

hand. She's just staring straight ahead and her face is all frozen.

My hand's still going, it's just squeezing, squeezing, like she's a melon, and her eyes are like, I don't know, they've got shutters over them, and after a while my hand just kind of stops moving because she's sitting there like a statue, and also because I remember what Chlo said about melons, and I can't think of anything else for my hand to do, and there's something about the way Dori's so still and quiet, staring straight ahead like she's got shutters over her eyes.

And finally, I get what they're saying. I thought you were my friend, those shutters are saying.

She'll let me do whatever I want. I know she will.

She just won't ever call me again.

And hey, that would be a good thing. Wouldn't it?

My hand feels stupid, just hanging there in her shirt, so I pull it out.

I almost want to say I'm sorry, but I don't know why and I don't know how.

She still hasn't moved. Hasn't said one syllable.

"If you don't want me to do that," I say, like it's all her fault, "you could *say* so."

She shrugs, like she's tired. "I forgot. It was stupid," she says, and she sounds tired too.

"What was stupid?"

"Guys always want sex." She shrugs again, shutters closed. "It's always part of the deal, isn't it? I forgot."

I don't know about that, but me, I never forgot that I wanted sex. Not for a moment. "You shouldn't have kept calling me," I tell her, loud enough to inform the duct-taped rabbit ears *and* the teapot curtains, too. I finally sit back on the couch, fold my arms across my chest. Because I don't know how to take it—her sitting there, not looking at me like that.

Like she thought it was enough, just talking to me on the phone—but now she knows it's not.

"No, I liked calling you." Her voice is small. "I just should have remembered."

"Yeah," I tell her. "You should have remembered."

"It was because you never talked like the other guys, when we were on the phone. You never talked nasty or anything."

"*You* talked on the phone. Not me."

She clears her throat. "The other guys wouldn't even talk to me at all. Jordan's the only one who acted like I was a human being. And even he—well. But you—I just thought you weren't like that."

"I *am* like that. All the time. I'm a lousy bastard. Everybody knows it."

She shrugs again, that tired shrug. "I don't think you're a lousy bastard. You want sex? Well, so does every other guy on the planet. I know I've heard you say mean stuff to people. But I always thought when people do that, it means they're hurting inside."

I'm just sitting there, arms still folded, but now I'm staring down at her with this horrible sinking feeling. Realizing what a mistake it was to ever, ever speak to her. I thought she was safe because she was a nobody, a slut, Jordan Palmer's seconds. And all the time the danger wasn't that she'd come up and talk to me in the hall.

It was that she'd say stuff like this and throw it in my face.

"I always figured," Dori says, "that you just wanted to hurt people before they hurt you."

It's the most terrible thing anybody's ever said to me. Jesus. My eyes actually start stinging. Shit.

I get up. "I gotta go." My voice is thick. I head for the door. At least, I think I'm heading for the door. My eyes are blurry.

"Colt. Wait. I didn't mean to make you cry."

"I'm not *crying*," I tell her. "I'm *leaving*."

"Colt." She puts her hand on my arm. "You're a guy and all. But if you were as lousy as the rest of them, you wouldn't have stopped with just feeling me up."

Now let me tell you what a lousy bastard I am. Her hand is warm on my arm, and behind this panicked feeling that I gotta run, the back of my mind is clicking—Wait, Colt!

Use this! Play her, let her put her arms around you. And before you know it *she'll* be doing *you*.

I'm looking down the barrel of an extremely easy pity fuck! Take that, Grace!

But somehow Dori has finished up what Chlo started. Dori has let the rest of the air out of me. This basketball is flatter than a pancake. All the shitty things I've ever done have come back and piled on me today. They're all weighing me down so much that I can't take doing even one more shitty thing.

I'm actually almost looking ahead for once, and what I see is that if I do this thing, what I'll remember for the rest of my life is how I felt like a total turd afterward. Hell, I feel like a turd right now, even just thinking about it. The afterward, I mean.

So for once I follow through on something I know I should do.

"I've got to go." I pull away, make it to the door. Push the screen open a little before I turn around. She's still standing in the middle of the room. Dori and her breasts. "I can't be trusted," I tell her. "I know me, and I'm telling you. *Don't ever trust me.*"

She doesn't move—she's standing in the middle of the carpet, her hands at her sides. She can't argue my point, since she knows I came over for the sole purpose of screwing her.

"Maybe not in person," she says. "But what about over the phone?"

That surprises me. I don't know what to say to that. Jesus, I don't know what to think of this girl. Finally I manage to croak, "I dunno. Maybe." Then I shrug, and I walk out her door.

The screen door bangs shut behind me. The grass is long; it swishes against my shoes as I walk back across the lawn. I didn't get laid, not even close—but still everything seems different from when I went in.

I get into the car. The sun's heading toward the horizon. I drive away, knowing for sure that I am never coming back.

All I can say is I picked a really stupid time to grow up.

CHAPTER TWELVE

One of the Other Million People in the World

The way home is very weird. A lot has happened in a very short amount of time. And what's strange is that just a little while ago I couldn't stand another second of Chlo being around, but now I think I might want to be with somebody who's not going to stare at my stapled face, but who's going stare at a book instead while my mouth spills out everything that's happened to me today. Who's then going to say one sentence without even looking up, one sentence that'll make everything clear, and then I'll understand everything that's happened.

I'm thinking all this, I can't shake this feeling, and when I get home I head for the phone. I'm even about to pick it up before I realize that not only do I not know Chlo's phone number, I don't even know her last name.

It pretty much figures. Who else could sit alone with

somebody in a room for weeks and weeks and not even know her name?

I'm standing with one hand on the phone, thinking all this, when it rings under my hand.

It scares the holy shit out of me. For one thing, it's loud. For another, there's a million people I don't want to talk to right now, and one person that I do.

Chlo.

Every other time I've picked up the stupid phone— every time I ever wanted to talk to one person—it was always one of the other million people in the world calling me. So what are the odds on this, the shittiest day of my life?

I pick it up. "Hello?" My voice is shaking.

"Trammel? That you?"

It's Chlo.

I open my mouth—and for the first time in my life, I can't think of one damn thing to say.

"You there?" Chlo says.

"Yeah," I say, and my voice sounds like rusty nails.

"Just wanted to make sure you got home okay."

"Yeah. I did."

"Seemed like you had sort of a bad day."

"This has been," I tell her, getting my voice back, "the most extremely shitty day of my life."

"Uh-huh. Well. I didn't call to invite myself to a pity

party. I called for two reasons. One, because I've been thinking about why I was staying there with you in the nurse's office."

That's a good point. Why did she stay there with me?

"You're no bowl of cherries, Trammel. You're selfish. And you can be pretty mean. But like I said, I like you okay, and I think part of that is because I have this gut feeling that way down deep on the inside—waaaay deep down—you have the *seed* of a good heart."

"Great," I tell her. "Thanks for trying to pump me up here."

"And I was thinking, Trammel, that since I like you okay, and you've got the seed of a good heart, and since you had the most extremely shitty day of your life, that I am going to make at least a somewhat half-hearted attempt to get your mind off your troubles, as a gesture of friendship. Knowing, of course, that you'll probably laugh in my face. Please understand that I'm not asking you on a date," she adds, "but I was going to a movie tonight, and since my usual crew is all busy—including my boyfriend, you hear that, Trammel? My *boyfriend*, whom I love with all my heart, is busy. So I was wondering if you, whom I merely like okay, would like to come with me. As a friend. Just keeping things straight here," she adds. "And feel free to say no. It won't hurt my feelings a bit."

"What movie?" I ask.

"*1900.*"

For a second I'm not sure whether she's telling me the time or the title.

"It's by Bernardo Bertolucci," Chlo says, as if that explains something.

I start to say, "Oh yeah, him." But I don't bother—Chlo'll know I'm lying. All I know is it's got to be one of those artsy-fartsy things. One of those *La Behhhllle* things.

"It's at TMU, so you're supposed to be a student. But they never check IDs. It's only two bucks to get in. And we'd be going dutch, Trammel. You got that?"

"Yeah."

Silence.

"So, you want to go?"

"I guess."

Silence.

"You sure you're okay, Trammel?"

"Yeah."

"You're awfully quiet. And well-mannered. For you."

"Sorry."

Silence.

"So what do you think?"

"About what?"

"About anything. About going to a movie. About

Bertolucci's oeuvre. About your most extremely shitty day."

What do I think? I'm thinking about Grace. How can she not see that she's just another in a long line of Doris and Graces?

I'm thinking maybe stupid isn't just not knowing what a metaphor is.

"You know those dead guys who wrote all that English?" I burst out. "Like Byron and Keats and them? I think maybe they only wrote all that stuff in the first place because they wanted to get in some girl's pants. Or somebody's pants, anyway," I add, remembering Byron the letch.

"Maybe so," Chlo says. "Anyway, sounds like you're ready for that English test."

"Those dead guys," I tell Corinne, "those dead guys don't know shit about romance."

WEEK SIX

CHAPTER THIRTEEN

What I Know

The movie was actually pretty good, although it was a little long. It had this evil Nazi guy, and at one point two guys got naked with one girl. On the way home Corinne told me how her green hair got her kicked out of Country Valley Prep School—because it turns out that Corinne is not poor, not at all—and then she went to Trinity Academy for the beginning of this year, until she got the boot when she refused to wear the uniform. She told me how she got her hair cut because it had lost its shock value with her stepmother. And that Brian still doesn't really like it.

I didn't tell her what I was really thinking—that Brian better watch his ass. Corrine's not the type to sit around and take shit from anybody, and old Bri is really starting to dish it out. Telling his own girlfriend how to do her hair.

What I told her was how I pitched three no-hitters last year on the freshman team, and how I think I might want to go to UT or Notre Dame. Corinne said she'd come to one of my games sometime. I told her a little bit about Dori.

I talked about Grace too.

The next week is the English test. I didn't study for it, of course. I grip my pen and start writing what I know. It doesn't take long.

1. Name two characteristics of Romantic poetry and give at least one example of each characteristic by discussing the poem in which it appears.

I do'nt know any characteristics of romantic poety. But I can tell what poems I liked and why and what poets. I liked them all okay accept Keats becuase he was boreing. He did'nt have affares and he was'nt an athist. The poems I liked best were the one by Woolsworth about studying outside. I thougt took him to many words to say a simple idea. I like the idea, but it should have been shorter. She Walks In Beauty the one about Bryon's cousin who wore a black dress with dimonds to a party. I liked it becuase

I know how that feels, it reminds me of a girl I use to go out with. But I aslo think Bryon probaly only wrote that just to look smart anyway becuase he went with alot of woman and other peopel not just his cousin. I aslo liked Ozymandyas by Shelly. The one about the statu that fell down and got covered up by sand becuase it makes me wonder what this scholl will be like in a thosand years. And what will be left of me for people to see. Probaly not much, acording to Shelly!

I do'nt like poems very much but I guess I like these okay.

I realize it won't get me a passing grade. It didn't in biology. Nobody's interested in what I know, just what they can teach me. But *I'm* interested in what I know. Because it takes me a long time to learn it.

Note at the top of test paper, English, period 4:

Colt, it's good to see you trying to do your own thinking for a change.

75

Poem from the journal of Corinne Hecht:

The Pitcher

He marks the mound as his.
Prowls, struts, commands,
demands all eyes,
then, satisfied,
begins.

His body stills
face stone
mouth firm
eyes hard
he coils up likeawhipthen
crack! *unfurls the ball . . .*
Smack! *leather on leather.*

Then, satisfied,
turns
to smile
a lazy, muscled smile
at all those captive eyes.